Nephilim

by Wade Thomas

STONE TABLE BOOKS

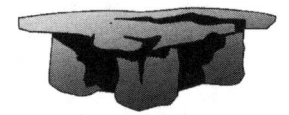

NEPHILIM

Copyright ©Wade Thomas 2022. All rights reserved. Except for brief quotations in critical publications or reviews, no part of this book may be reproduced in any manner without prior written permission from the publisher. Write: Permissions, Wipf and Stock Publishers, 199 W, 8th Ave., Suite 3 Eugene, OR 97401.

Stone Table Books
An Imprint of Wipf and Stock Publishers
199 W, 8th Ave., Suite 3
Eugene, OR 97401

PAPERBACK ISBN: 978-1-6667-3649-6
HARDCOVER ISBN: 978-1-6667-9484-7
EBOOK ISBN: 978-1-6667-9485-4

Cataloguing-in-Publication entry is available from the National Library of Australia
http://catalogue.nla.gov.au.
This edition first published in 2022

Typesetting by Ben Morton.
Cover photo by Edward Howell on Unsplash

For Sunshine.

"The last enemy that shall be destroyed is death."
First Corinthians 15:26

Acknowledgments

This story would not have been possible without my children, who listened to it and loved it right along with me, nor without my wife, who makes our home possible. Thank you Ellie, Wade, Zoey, AnaLucia, Judah, Azariah, and Sarah, my bride.

I would also like to thank Mark Worthing for his literary assistance, and Holly Carraher for some welcome encouragement.

Characters

1892

Raymond Stanton – Widower, new resident of Sunbury, father of Rachel

Rachel Stanton – Young Christian woman, daughter of Raymond

Josiah Hall – Doctor, bachelor, lifelong member of Sunbury's Presbyterian Church

Hannibal Guthridge – Aged resident of Sunbury, known for quarrelsomeness

Noel Flagler – Sunbury's lone vocational policeman, married father of two young boys

Ed Aimes – Farmer, married father, member of Presbyterian Church, neighbor of Hannibal Guthridge

Bill Kline – Farmer, member of Presbyterian Church, voluntary assistant to Noel Flagler

Joe Mertz – Farmer, hunter, friend of Noel Flagler

Abigail Tufts – Dressmaker, married but childless, member of Presbyterian Church

Reverend Francis Lowell – Pastor of Presbyterian Church, bachelor

1843

Marvin Branson – Confidence man, traveling the American northeast as a supposed spiritualist

Theodore McCabe – Marvin Branson's secret partner

Harold and June Bloomfield – Proprietors of Sunbury Inn

Sidney Seagram – Trustee, founder of Sunbury Bank

Prologue

Sunbury, Massachusetts – 1892

The dog was wandering in the middle of the dirt road about a five-minute walk outside of town. In its short life, some 971 days to be exact, it had witnessed several interesting things. Being a dog, though, none had actually registered in its brain. It had once, for instance, passed an envoy from the Governor, which was noteworthy enough in its own right, but made even more so by the fact that the man was coughing uncontrollably and only three days away from dying of consumption.

But in the life of a stray dog notable political personalities and the occasional hanging (it had been an unaware spectator to *two* hangings already) are not nearly as compelling as a discarded fish or a cluster of ungnawed chicken bones. And this was one of those fortunate nights when this particular dog in this particular Massachusetts village had been able to sniff out the leg bone of a chicken which had given its life so that the Miller family could have a gracious Sabbath dinner. It was now carrying the bone happily along this dirt road on the outer rim of the town, gripping it with all the tactile canine joy it had between its teeth as it heard what to it amounted to a threat. It instantly perked up and turned towards the moonlight being poured over the open green to its right.

Nephilim

Across the dirt road the ground rose a few feet and then flattened suddenly. From there, it stretched out for several hundred yards to the woods that surrounded the village. Taking up much of that flat ground looking from where the dog stood now, bracing and with its ears straight up over his head, was Sunbury's cemetery. Fresh earth covered two graves, graves not connected in what we might call the proper sense, but which had each this night been subject to what the dog was now hearing.

It instinctively backed up to the other side of the road when the sound grew faster and louder, sensing that whatever it was might soon be after it and what it had between his teeth. But after a few seconds of increasing intensity the sound suddenly stopped. Then, the dog watched as a shadow sped away from the second pile of earth it had engaged in the cemetery that night and into the woods just out of the reach of the half-moon's light.

After a few seconds the dog ran off in the other direction, carrying its bone with it, knowing full well what digging was, but not having the slightest idea what could have been so appealing in there.

1

1892

Raymond Stanton owned three things that he valued enough to think of with any sort of moment as he set up his new home in Sunbury. The family Bible, faded with almost equal parts age and use and currently laying on the kitchen table. His rifle, leaning in the corner of his bedroom. And his wedding band, locked on his left ring finger where it would stay for as long as he had left. He was just sentimental enough to lament the fact that it was his second rifle.

Morning number forty-two in Sunbury. He took a moment to scratch out as much to his brother.

Freddy,

I have found the friend about whom you spoke so often. He remembers you well. He told me something interesting about father and your Jane, something I'll have to tell you in person if I am to give it full merit.

Sunbury is pleasant.

Give my best to Jane and Winnie.

Raymond

He didn't like the word pleasant, but there it was, and the time had come to move on to the next task.

"Rachel?"

His daughter answered and came in through the front door a moment later.

"I'm going into town to send off some letters and place an order for oil. I believe I'll stop in at Mrs. Tufts' and pick up your dress. Do you recall if she told you it would be ready?"

Rachel nodded." She did say Monday afternoon, but I expect if you came by today she could finish it and give it to you." She smiled and Raymond's chest tightened a bit. Rose, his wife, had died ten months ago, and when Rachel smiled trimly like that, with just a slight narrowing of the eyes and the left corner of her lips drawing up enough to satisfy a dim echo of happiness, she looked very much like her mother. She resembled her in a way Raymond had never known was possible until Rachel began approaching the age Rose had been when he'd married her. Rachel was herself, and yet in being that while also being Rose's daughter, she was simultaneously a window into Rose he hadn't had before.

Rose and Joshua had died four days apart. She had died first, and that had never ceased seeming strange for Raymond. It had been Joshua who had gotten sick first, and he seemed to suffer more than his mother. But one afternoon Raymond had come home and seen Rose on the floor of the front room of their small Boston house. She died later that night amidst the sound of coughing like nothing he'd ever heard. He'd

Chapter 1

prayed constantly, most of the night resting his head on the edge of their bed where he'd carried her. Joshua lay in the other bedroom, sleeping the entire day and night away for the second time in as many days. Rachel had been in Providence, by the grace of Almighty God, for three months, helping Rose's sister with her newborn baby and her specially affected small daughter, four-year-old Claudia. The doctor came several hours after Raymond had laid Rose in the bed and told Raymond several things he already knew. Pastor Scotts had come as well. He had come to the parish only four months prior, and they didn't know each other with any depth or breadth yet, but he composed himself well for the moment. Raymond could now only remember two or three things he'd said in the hour or so he'd sat in the bedroom with the two of them. The lamp in the corner of the room had fought with a dusk that had had no moon, and before long Pastor Scotts was only a shadow against the wall as he prayed in a hoarse voice, whispering to the Almighty whose grace they shared that He might spare her for her husband's sake and for her children's, and for the church's and for their neighbors'. Rose had been a blessing to the several widows on their street, two of whom had been members with them at St. Andrew's. Madeleine, the seventy-three-year-old woman whose husband had died more than thirty years ago was particularly close to Rose. Hardly a day passed without them spending an hour in conversation about nearly anything under the sun, and Rose delighted in the remnants of the old woman's French accent, mentioning to Raymond more than once that since French had such a musical sound, she must learn it one day.

His wife and his young son had died. And now they were here, what remained of the Stantons, and he had letters to send, and oil to purchase, and Rachel's dress to retrieve. He let himself close his eyes for two or three seconds, and collect his strength, and then he returned his daughter's smile.

Raymond's faith still stood, by God's mercy, and by his own prayers. Sunbury was a new home, his and Rachel's, now that they were together again. They had already become members of Sunbury's Presbyterian Church. He lay no blame for the death of his wife at the feet of God, though the grief was perhaps hotter now than even at first. To lose little Joshua so soon after Rose, and then, after much prayer and consideration and due fasting, to settle in a new place with only half formed hopes, he now had a sharper sense of all that had been lost. But grief and doubt were not the same, and he mourned with faith.

"Would you-" but Raymond stopped as he saw what he was fairly certain was their neighbor, Miles Cartwright, running past their front window and looking quickly behind him, a look of concern and, at first glance, even dread on his face. And then four more

Chapter 1

figures ran by their house, headed west, in the direction leading out of town.

Rachel turned and looked out their window, too, realizing her father was staring at something, but no more neighbors passed by. As Raymond and she stepped out of their front door and went around the north side of the house and looked west, they saw two dozen or so of their neighbors running up the rise in the ground outside of town and into the cemetery.

* * *

Sunbury is a pleasant village.

We have been attending Sunbury's Presbyterian Church, and the minister here, a Reverend Lowell, is very appealing and gracious. I have been touched during his sermons on more than one occasion, particularly this past Lord's Day as he preached from Habakkuk.

I have struck up quite an acquaintance with the wife of a shopkeeper, a Mrs. Abigail Tufts. She is preparing a dress for me for our trip to Uncle Simon's and Aunt Joan's, and I have found her delightfully witty. She is a very forthright and gregarious woman, having no children and, I suppose, having had much more time and energy to devote to cultivating her inner graces. Though perhaps I shouldn't assume so much. I'd rather say that she is sly and humorous and hasn't the slightest pretension of being above anyone or anything in the world, and I have been drawn to her as almost no other woman I've ever known. Besides dear Mother, of course.

You asked me about Father, and I want to be delicate in my answer, not from fear that you will not be gracious in interpreting what I say, but in that I don't know if I can adequately explain all my thoughts about him. There is no man like my father that I can imagine. He is steadfast and faithful to me in his love and admiration in a way I cannot imagine being exceeded by another father to his daughter. I have not the slightest doubt that I am in his utmost consideration in all that he decides and puts forth his efforts in. Yet there is some sadness, some grief or quiet fear or unutterable loss that he cannot share with me or with anyone, and in the moments when I am most aware of it, I sense that almost everything else in this world has become less real to him. There was a night not long ago when I came into the front room of our new house to see him staring out the window as he polished his rifle, and it seemed to me he was looking down towards the ground and examining the reflection of his rifle in the window. I didn't want to startle him and so gently called for him in barely a whisper. He turned immediately, but didn't seem to recognize me for a moment. In those few seconds before he became father again, I saw a despair in his face, a longing or fright; a melancholy that I had never seen before and hope to never see again. I love him so dearly, and this is agony to see.

I dare not dwell too much on the hardships of a man who is so thoroughly devoted to being a good citizen and Christian. Do not think that what I say here is more frequent than his charity or great acts of longsuffering, such as spending all day yesterday

Chapter 1

chopping wood for our nearly destitute elderly neighbor, Mr. Parkinson. Father is as much a wonder in his love for his fellow man as ever.

Pray for him, and for me, in that I may be the daughter he needs.

Yours Truly,
Rachel

2
1892

Just as Bill Kline, the first of the crowd to arrive at the cemetery, was pushing his hat up over his hairline and whistling, unsure exactly what he was looking at but knowing it was neither natural nor good, Hannibal Guthridge was swearing up a storm. He had stepped out the backdoor of his old farmhouse and seen the door to his barn ajar.

If one of Ed Aimes' young sons had snuck in there again and stolen eggs from his hens just to use them as projectiles at the other (unsuspecting) brother, he would skin them alive. What infuriated him even more was Ed's inexplicable ambivalence about his sons' recklessness and lack of respect for the property of others. It wasn't like Ed was a drinker like old Tommy Judson on the other side of Hannibal's property. Tommy was a different kind of problem altogether, and Hannibal could almost excuse the old man's ill temper and the fact that he let that pup he had yap at all hours and run loose all over the village. Almost excuse him right now when he was mad at the Aimes family, anyway. But as Hannibal's nearly two-minute walk out to his barn ended, hampered by early morning stiffness of too many varieties of ailment to lament in words (though he'd try, given a listening ear, as the men down at the General Store could attest), he came to the cold

Chapter 2

realization that Ed Aimes' boys had nothing to do with why his barn door was open.

Troublemakers they were, but horse thieves they were not. And sure enough, his five-year-old work horse was gone.

By this time Bill Kline and the other two dozen or so people who had gathered at the cemetery had found Hannibal's horse. It was ripped open at the belly and with most of its insides stretched across the wet grass growing over the graves. Its body was more or less equidistant between two graves that had been dug up, and by now Forrest Jones and Bill had each looked in both and seen the empty coffins laying at the bottom amidst layers of dark, damp earth. Bill was a simple corn farmer, and he'd never been outside the state of Massachusetts, but he was sensible and respected in the town, and so he figured that it was his job to take a look at whatever this was first.

There had only been one murder in Sunbury's history as an incorporated village, and it had been the result of two-and-a-half bottles of whiskey and one-and-a-half generations of feuding about the property line between the Jacksons and the Ewings. The perpetrator had been tried, convicted, and hanged with the passing of only one Lord's Day. From that moment on, the extent of criminal activity in town had been limited to an annual game of high stakes poker hosted by Joseph Lansing in his parlor amidst cigar smoke and brandy glasses and a pair of counterfeiting brothers who ended up running out of town on a Saturday night and being caught in Baltimore on Monday morning.

What Bill Kline and his neighbors had discovered that Monday morning in the cemetery was criminal in more ways than they could count. But the criminality of what they came across was not their chief concern. There is something uniquely unholy about the desecration of a grave. We know what life is, we know its value, and among the ways we take count of that value is our treatment of the body after life has left it. Anointing for burial, aromatic spices, newly cut tombs, prayers over the burial ground, not standing on top of it; all of these gestures are in keeping with what we know to be true. The fact that Laura Atwood and David Steatham's graves had been dug up, their coffins broken open, and their bodies stolen for reasons unknown left every one of the two dozen citizens of Sunbury standing in the morning grass morally nauseated.

Josiah Hall, the local doctor, forty-one years old with red hair and an unassuming demeanor despite all his seriousness, spat into the grass to his right and thought something that, to that point, only he had. The sun was up behind them all by now, and the carcass of the animal lay right out in the open. He could see plainly enough, even at twenty paces, that there were no teeth marks on it anywhere, no sign of mauling or

Chapter 2

tearing away of flesh. The horse had just simply been gutted. Josiah almost always had seven thoughts for every one word he spoke. If anyone had been inclined to ask him what he was thinking, staring as he was without blinking and with his brow furrowed, his red eyebrows inching downward in ever deeper concentration, he would have said, "I'm not sure yet." But no one was so inclined. Bill Kline had asked someone to fetch Sunbury's only vocational policeman, Noel Flagler. Until Noel got here, Bill felt the need to at least confirm that no remains of any kind were left in either coffin, which he was able to do without much trouble.

"Is this some kind of witchcraft?" Ed Aimes asked the cluster of people in earshot of him. He never took his eyes off of the mounds of earth on the western side of Laura Atwood's grave. It was a fair question, but no one had an answer to it, so it died in the air. No one else spoke until Noel came bounding across the dirt road and said, "Lord help us" when he saw the crimson stain covering the wet grass of a good portion of the cemetery between the two graves.

"What are we looking at, Bill?"

"I'm not at all sure, Noel." He scratched his hairline, still exposed from when he'd pushed his hat up. "We've had two graves robbed, Laura Atwood's and David Steatham's. This horse was laid out here dead. Somebody or something just ripped it right open."

"It's Hannibal Guthridge's horse," Forrest Jones offered. He was now standing closer to the road, having instinctively pushed himself away from the graves.

"Can somebody go get him?" Noel asked, and when no one volunteered he looked over at Ed Aimes, knowing they were neighbors. Ed nodded without a word, but he didn't look any too happy about being sent on the errand.

"There's no sign of Mrs. Atwood or Mr. Steatham?" Noel asked Bill and Forrest, seeing as they appeared to be the leaders of the little discovery party.

Bill shook his head, then wiped his brow with his right arm. He left a small trail of mud up near his hairline. He suddenly had the urge to get sick, but he was able to hold it down by focusing on a dandelion growing five feet away over his aunt's grave.

Noel put his hands in his trouser pockets and scratched his right leg deeply in an effort to get his thoughts in order. Just before he drew blood he was settled that the ordinary brand of tomfoolery you got from local boys or even drunken millworkers from neighboring Fairhaven was ruled out. Stealing a horse would have been normal for that sort, maybe even killing it, but gutting it and leaving the carcass in the middle of a cemetery seemed far beyond the standard rowdy boyhood fare. And digging up two graves would

Chapter 2

have taken all night and would have been hard work for even a couple of men. The liquor would have worn off long before the job was done. And that assumed that such young men looking for mischief would have settled on digging up newly buried bodies from a cemetery. Unlikely.

Noel pulled his hands back out of his pockets and ran the fingers of his right hand through his sandy yellow mustache for a moment instead of digging them into his thigh.

"Joe, would you go get your hound?"

Joseph Mertz nodded, and ran across the road towards his street, where his wife would be just putting away the breakfast dishes. Joe was always glad to help, and his bloodhound and a few men out in the woods on the western edge of the cemetery would be a start. Noel was trying to picture in his mind the sort of a man who would have no problem spending all night unearthing two bodies, hoping that starting at the solution to the equation and working backwards would help. After a few seconds he found it didn't. He couldn't picture any such man. Or men. And the mess of a dead animal in the middle of the grass just made it that much harder.

"Bill? Forrest? I believe we'd best take Joe and his dog out into those woods here and see what we can find. We can help Hannibal tend to the animal when we're back."

"Noel? Would you mind if I joined you?"

It was Dr. Hall.

Noel nodded without unfurrowing his brow. He was unsure why the doctor would want to come, but he was a prudent enough man to know that there was no good reason to turn him down. The four of them bided their time until Joe returned with his red-brown hound trotting across the dirt and into the dew and thick turf of the cemetery. Joe's bowler hat flew off as he anxiously bounded the last few steps, and he turned around quickly to pick it up, his dog halting beside him for a moment before sniffing at Mary Ellen Howser's leg. She was a good sport about it but was obviously happy when Joe had his hat back on his head and had joined Noel up with Bill and Forrest a moment later. The rest of the bystanders stood and watched, unable to walk away from the sheer strangeness of this thing.

Dr. Hall came up slowly behind the other four men. He made note of something that made him stop for a moment, and gave him a wide sort of unease.

Being untrained in the criminal sciences and trusting Noel for what he was worth as a village policeman, Dr. Hall brought it up in a low enough voice that only his four fellow investigators could hear.

"Noel? There aren't any wagon tracks or any disturbed earth, like there would be if the bodies were dragged."

Chapter 2

Noel stopped and looked from left to right across the cemetery. The thing had actually occurred to him, too, but he'd hoped to see something a little further southwest, closer to the woods. It was clear now from where they stood that nothing had been ridden or dragged across the grass that night.

"It seems they were carried off."

The spectral thought of a creature carrying off Mrs. Atwood and Mr. Steatham in its arms or over its shoulder was unsettling, but after a moment all four men and one dog continued their trudge across the grass and towards the shadows under the trees. It was six steps for Josiah when they heard the scream coming from town, back from what sounded to be near Hannibal Guthridge's property.

* * *

The severed hand was lying next to the bottom step at the back of Hannibal's house, soaked in slowly drying red blood. Ed Aimes, no longer attached to that right hand, had his back against the wall of the house as he turned his head back and forth and mumbled incoherently. His face was the color of new bone, and his hair was sweaty and stuck to his forehead as though he he'd just stepped out of a cloudburst.

"What happened!" Noel shouted it, which was unsettling to the men who'd run with him and to the handful of others who had cautiously followed because a bloodcurdling scream in the middle of the morning is something with a particularly powerful gravitational pull.

What had happened was that Hannibal Guthridge had had it in a very hellish sort of way, which would soon make more sense. Something about the way Ed Aimes had started the conversation had made it obvious to Hannibal that not only was he happy about his horse being slaughtered like a pig, but that he was involved. And that horse was a part of Hannibal's livelihood, serving as his carrier and transporter of anything heavier than a sack of apples. Something about those green eyes of Ed's seeming to be just looking for a smile to sit over made Hannibal decide insanity was a much more desirable option than buying a new horse and getting on with life. And so, after leaving the room for less than a minute to fetch his axe, Hannibal had returned and given Ed a good enough scare to get him out into the back yard. But then Ed had stopped to try to tell him just one more time that they'd found his horse, which, as far as Hannibal was concerned, was the last straw. Down came the axe, and there went Ed, down into the grass with a scream like Hannibal had never heard.

And Hannibal had smiled the whole time.

* * *

Chapter 2

The birds didn't come near it. Two crows had been circling overhead, but now that it was back to the clearing and picking up Mrs. Atwood and Mr. Cheatham, they had flown away south as though a hurricane were chasing them. It had Mrs. Atwood over its left shoulder, Mr. Cheatham over its right. The forest floor was clear of undergrowth here, where the shadows under the twelve-foot rock wall were long most of the day. It was only bare, moist earth under its feet, making almost no sound. Somewhere on the east side of the rock some water was dripping, and ten yards or so away a squirrel scampered to the top of a tree. Beyond those sounds, it was silent. There was no breeze.

It jumped to the top of the rock and set them both down.

The whispering would tell it what was next.

3

Sunbury, Massachusetts – 1843

Sometimes a man has an idea, and sometimes an idea has a man. In this case the man was Marvin Branson, and the idea was nested in the branches of a greed that had yet to even whiff satisfaction. It was no coincidence that Marvin Branson came to Sunbury when he did. Whether or not he was aware of it is largely irrelevant. What matters is that what he was selling was in high demand. That is, what he had in the satchel he carried with him in his right hand. A man's work is seldom as important to him as when it's all he has left, and Marvin had lived for years only one step away from just such a position. What he clung to now, what was in his simple brown satchel and waiting for the first best opportunity to come out and make the world shine and the money fall, was his best chance to save himself.

But first he needed a room.

Sunbury's Inn was quite a nice place to rent one. Mr. and Mrs. Harold Bloomfield had maintained it since June Bloomfield's father Gregory had died thirty-four years earlier and left it to his son-in-law. Both Harold and June were diligent, tidy, pleasant people who most guests found to be just the right degree of charming without being pretentious. Harold also kept a few crops on the property, which he tended with the love of a farmer who doesn't need to farm, and which

Chapter 3

June enjoyed as they kept him busy enough during the morning that she could savor some gossip with any female guests who might be staying. Both souls were as ripe for Marvin and what he brought as August cherries, though he didn't know that for at least the first three minutes. Harold did most of the talking, explaining that they had a room he could rent for four dollars a week, and that three meals a day were included. By the time June had hung up his coat and hat and asked what Mr. Branson was in Sunbury for, Marvin had known. But knowing was one thing, taking the opportunity was another entirely.

For now, Marvin merely said that he had some business to see to locally and that he planned on being in town for at least two weeks. He happily paid Mr. Bloomfield for both weeks in advance. Harold was surprised, but he didn't object. He was happy enough to have the eight dollars. He was also pleased with the fact that Mr. Branson struck him as a responsible man, one who would be in his room at a reasonable hour and perhaps even attend church services on Sunday. Harold himself didn't attend, but he was pleased with churchgoing men. They were less trouble.

Harold and June showed Marvin to his room on the second floor and advised him that they'd already had breakfast themselves, but that there was a tavern a short walk away that could serve him. Marvin simply smiled politely and told them that he'd had breakfast in nearby Plainfield before taking a coach to Sunbury. They told him they'd leave him to settle himself in and attend to his business, and as soon as the door was shut Marvin's smile changed. He set the satchel down on the small bed and narrowed his eyes. At least two, and they were the first two he'd met. He might only need ten. He pulled it out of the satchel and closed his eyes, and the smile grew a little, stretching up his left cheek. This would be a good week. He felt it. He lay down without even removing his tie or his shoes and fell fast asleep on the bed. There were no dreams.

4
1892

Ed Aimes was going to die. Dr. Hall, who'd applied a makeshift tourniquet as best he could, didn't want to say it out loud because it seemed half the town was standing on Hannibal's property staring at him right now. But he planned on telling Noel and Bill once he could get Ed back to his office, a half-mile away in the heart of town.

"Will you help me carry him?" Josiah looked up at Noel and squinted, the wrinkles at the outer edges of his green eyes flattening out and his red eyebrows standing out in the rising morning sun. Noel could tell it was serious by the way Dr. Hall wouldn't look away from him, and from the fact that there was no grimace or smile from his mouth. Dr. Hall was preparing for the inevitable, not for some serious medical work. Noel nodded, and grabbed Bill Kline's right arm, pulling him towards Ed Aimes. Noel put Ed's right arm over his own shoulders, not concerning himself about the blood. Bill took Ed's left arm, and they followed Dr. Hall as he stood up and made his way across Hannibal's property and towards town.

It was a ten-minute walk to Josiah Hall's office on Beadle Street. Noel brought Hannibal with them, had the old man walking angrily just in front of him, muttering a few words of protest with thirty seconds or so of silence in between. Hannibal's bald head somehow looked particularly sinister to Noel in this light. It had a putrid looking light brown mole about the size of the fingernail on Noel's ring finger, with a hair growing out of it a little off center. It bobbed up and down with Hannibal's head as he took his slow, irritable steps. The old, gray cuss was as angry as ever, angry at the man whose hand was laying back in his grass, and angry at the three men carrying his victim like a scarecrow through town as a handful of spectators stopped talking and walking just long enough to wonder at the fact that Ed Aimes could have ever had that much blood in him.

No worries, folks, Noel thought grimly. *I'm sure your blood will stay inside you most of the day today, and the rain will wash away his.*

Hannibal spat at the dirt to the right of Beadle Street as the men came up to Josiah Hall's office, and for reasons Noel couldn't identify, that's what gave him the final push into outrage.

"Hannibal!"

Hannibal looked over at Noel with fire in his eyes, and Noel's surprise at the total lack of any shame in the old man pleased Hannibal. He smiled, and spat again, this time right into Beadle Street, just in front of Noel's shoes. It took every strand of determination Noel had in him to not strangle the skinny old man right there in the street.

Chapter 4

"Carry him on in to that table right there," Dr. Hall directed Bill and Noel, and the weight of his deep voice was enough to take Noel's mind off of how much he hated Hannibal Guthridge right then.

Ed Aimes didn't weigh much as far as grown men go, but he was bearing none of his own weight at this point, so it was awkward for Noel and Bill to get him through the door and onto Josiah's table as gingerly as they could. Noel had no knowledge of physiology, but once Ed was on the table and he could see his face, he knew right away why Dr. Hall had sounded the way he had out at Hannibal's property. He knew he was going to have a hanging to administer soon.

Ed Aimes' whole face was the color of a young child's teeth, and it was drenched in sweat. The place where his right hand had been had spilled his blood all over his trousers, his shirt, his shoes. Dr. Hall was holding it up and looking at it the way an old woman might look at her patchwork. His brow was tight, his eyes narrowed, and he was weighing whatever his next steps would be.

"He's lost too much blood?" Noel asked.

Josiah didn't answer. He just stood up and walked to the left side of the room where he pulled out a few strips of clean, white cloth and a brown glass bottle. When he got back to Ed's side, he set to work quickly and methodically, cleaning the wound and applying the cloth bandages. Noel ran outside and vomited into

Beadle Street. He couldn't help it. He hated to do it, especially in front of Hannibal, but something in him had to get out. He supposed it had something to do with knowing now that Ed was dying. Seeing that gore there where a half-hour ago his right hand had been and knowing that simple blow from a stubborn old man was the end of Ed, it made the blood and the white bone of his wrist exposed there in the morning sunlight that was slipping into Josiah's office through his dirty windows that much more repulsive.

Noel stood up after he was through, wiped his mouth with his handkerchief, and opened the front door to Dr. Hall's office again. No one looked at him as he re-entered. They were all looking at Ed. Noel was surprised to see that Hannibal Guthridge looked *scared* now.

Noel was confused for a few seconds, then looked over at Ed himself. There was Josiah Hall sitting at Ed's side, reading out loud from an old brown book. And when he heard the words, Noel felt some of the heaviness of what was scaring Hannibal Guthridge. It was like smoke in the room, thick and hot, making it hard to breathe and harder to think.

"He is the image of the invisible God, the firstborn of all creation."

Invisible God? Was that in there? In the Bible? Something was shaking in Noel, and he didn't care for it. No believing man, he was disturbed by the feeling

Chapter 4

that there was more in that room than the five of them, that murder was a weightier thing than even a hanging could tell the world, and that something real was happening.

Josiah Hall read the rest of Paul's letter to the church at Colossae as Ed Aimes died on his table, and twin tears slid down Hannibal's ancient left cheek.

* * *

Raymond Stanton stepped into Mrs. Tufts' small parlor with all the ease of a housefly resting on the ear of a tomcat. Mrs. Tufts was a fine woman, but he was who he was, and she worked in dresses. It was simple mathematics.

"I don't suppose what happened overnight made its way to you, Mr. Stanton?"

He grimaced slightly. Something about the way she said his name made him feel as though the whole world pitied him for his wife dying. And pity was worse than despair. Despair left you with at least one thing you could live with. Pity robbed you blind.

He cornered the thought and dispatched it. "I don't believe so. Unless-" He felt a cold something run down his back, and it wasn't the last time that day that he had the sense that this had all happened before. "Was that what had so many folks running out past the western edge of town?"

Mrs. Tufts smiled and gave him a knowing look. It was hard to say what she meant by that. It was the same sort of look his mother might have given him years ago when he'd confessed that he did indeed hope marriage was in his future. Women often frustrated him, but never more so than when he respected them.

"What was it?"

"I do feel terrible about the dishonor of it all, but it was a few graves robbed overnight. I will just suppose it was a handful of boys up to no good after having a bit too much whiskey, and I do hope they're caught and spend a good deal of time locked up and ashamed for it."

Raymond had no idea why his head felt lopsided, unbalanced all of a sudden, but it did, and as she told him about the dead horse and that it was at the very least, the graves of Laura Atwood and David Steatham, he sat down.

"Are you all right?"

"Yes." Then, "I'm not sure."

"What's wrong, Mr. Stanton?"

"My wife- Rose- She died of the fever, too. The same as Mrs. Atwood and Mr. Steatham." Was it that, simply? He decided it was.

"I'm sorry, I didn't realize. I can't imagine that's a very easy thing to bear, with or without a silly old woman bothering you with morning gossip. Let me get you some coffee."

Chapter 4

She came back a moment later carrying a small cup of black coffee and he took it gratefully, staring at the chestnut desk in her parlor where she had put Rachel's dress down a moment ago. That dress was striking, green like ivy in the shade. It reminded him of something. He strained to recall what it was.

"It was fairly recently, wasn't it, Mr. Stanton?"

"Yes." He took a sip of the coffee she'd brought him. He didn't say any more, not because he was frustrated with the topic as much as from the fact that he was still disoriented. What was happening?

"They truly have no idea who removed the bodies?"

Abigail Tufts shook her head, staring at his face with the most tender of concern. That was the moment Abigail Tufts decided to look in after Raymond Stanton from time to time. She kept that promise to herself, hidden in her heart, for as long as she could.

"I can pay you for the dress now if you don't mind," he said, taking one more sip of the coffee and then standing up. For a moment he thought that he would lose consciousness because of the dizziness that he suddenly felt thick around him and over him, but he stiffened his legs and resolved to keep himself alert and make his way over to Josiah Hall's office. He had struck up a very satisfying friendship with the doctor. They had met through the church, and his forthrightness and the steadiness and seriousness of his faith had earned him Raymond's profound admiration.

He clenched his teeth so hard they hurt, nodded at Mrs. Tufts, and paid for the dress. She gave it to him with thoughtfulness that didn't go unnoticed, and then told him to take care. Raymond stepped out into the street and felt the rising morning sun was a bit too bright for some reason. Only twice in his life had he had this particular sensation, and both times it proved to correspond to something momentous.

At roughly the same time of day that Marvin Branson had had his idea, Raymond Stanton put his foot onto the street and had the most unshakeable image of his wife's face, her green eyes lit up like fireflies under the shadows of trees at dusk, and just as impossible to hold onto. She was smiling with all the warmth and beauty that he missed more than he could tell Rachel, and the longing was somehow sweeter than even the having had been. He'd stopped walking, but he wasn't conscious of the fact that Mrs. Tufts was watching him through her window to his left or Madeleine Booker, whom he didn't even know, from across the street in front of Edward Hope's tailoring shop, where she had been picking up a suit for her son Matthew. Raymond felt within him the settled sadness that he would never hold Rose's face against his left shoulder again. He wasn't sure how a man could be so aware of something so painful and still walk and

Chapter 4

breathe and order oil and go to see his friend and have a talk. Rose's face was gone as quickly as it had come, and he wasn't sure how he could do anything right now.

Once he did what men do when they don't recover but have to keep walking, his first thought was Rachel. It always was. What did his grief mean for what was next for her? What if these moments began to happen more and more? What if one day he found he couldn't make himself get out of the bed to tend to the chores, buy the food, chop wood?

What some men thought about dollars and cents Raymond now thought about moments. There were things that lasted, but his marriage to Rose wasn't one of them. And that was the ache that held him in the middle of Doral Street now. Soured by the sense of something being misplaced. Out of joint.

Rachel happened to be praying then, because somebody really does run the world. She had no earthly idea why, but her heart was suddenly stung, kneeling at the head of her little bed with its thin beige blanket. She put her head down on that blanket, her face was wet now. She couldn't bear the weight of what she was suddenly sure was her father's pain. Rachel knew what it was to lose a mother, but she did not know what it was to lose half your body. Her father was wounded, and she wept from the hot sense that his eyes only told a quarter of the story, sunken and violet as they were. He had no one to tell, because her mother would have been the one to tell. He couldn't sleep because her weight wasn't in the bed with him, couldn't eat because hers was the food he'd grown accustomed to, couldn't smile because she was the one he smiled most for, couldn't laugh because her brightness and her gentle wit had been what he'd most laughed at. Somehow Rachel had missed all of the precision of this and, until now, and had just seen a widower's grief.

So she petitioned her Heavenly Father to help her earthly father sleep and eat and smile and laugh and trust, and she found herself unable to stop the sobbing that accompanied the prayers like the aroma that follows the flower. The house was empty and it was mid-morning, and somehow that made her feel more free to say out loud what she might never have had she been praying her normal evening prayers.

"I am afraid he will want to die, Father. That he will not want morning to come any longer."

And it was the truth, and as she prayed it to the Lord she was convinced would listen to her, her father found some inexplicable strength in his limbs and continued his walk to Beadle Street, where he went into his friend Dr. Josiah Hall's office to find a dead man on his table and the murderer crying in a chair by the window.

5

1843

Sunbury was more or less laid out as a circle, tucked neatly against a million acres of forest that lapped at the cemetery and Miles Gabbard's farm at the western edge of town. The woods would have been a part of the charm of the village if they were a different kind of woods, and Sunbury a different kind of village. But the dark creature that had roamed under those shadows had been known by a different name in a different time, and while no one in town remembered or even knew of what it had done, what it had started as, in years past, some shade of awareness and fear had held its place in their senses. I don't claim to know how it is a man who has never known that a murder occurred at a certain place can nonetheless find himself stopping for a moment, the hair at the base of his neck rising up, wondering why the spot where he's standing suddenly feels poisoned. Millennia ago, Jacob saw angels descending and knew he stood on holy soil. But not all angels are loyal angels, and some soil is infected.

Forty-nine years before what happened the morning Noel Flagler and Josiah Hall and the rest decided to step into the woods and look for Mrs. Atwood and Mr. Steatham, a man named Lucas Bentham had been drinking much more than his wife thought a good idea. Lucas was an angry man, and something his neighbor had said caused him to fire his rifle across his property and into his neighbor's barn, at which point his wife had taken the gun and pushed him out their backdoor. He'd thought about banging on the door or breaking one of his own windows, but in his tattered remnants of reasoning he decided instead to urinate on his wife's favorite flower bed and then go for a walk.

Lucas' property had been roughly the same plot as Miles Gabbard's, laying just south of the cemetery and butting up against the last hundred yards or so of tall grass and shrubbery before the trees began. His walk, more a stumble by the end, took him through that grass and up to a twenty-foot maple tree, where he put his right hand on the old wood of the trunk and vomited on his shoes. He laughed, even though nothing seemed funny to him at that point, then decided that he felt well enough to go for a night walk in the woods.

But even sober, Lucas Bentham's coordination was somewhere between a four-year-old's and a blind man's, which is why his shot into his neighbor's barn hadn't hit the cow that he'd intended but instead pinged off the roof, and why ten yards or so into the woods he tripped on nothing but flat ground and saw sparks as his head, sweaty and still smelling of vomit, thumped the soil under another maple tree.

Lucas was conscious enough to hear a few dead leaves be crushed under its feet but drunk enough to

Chapter 5

not feel the need to move and look at it. His face was towards the cemetery, which was somewhere out there in the half-moon's light. And so it was standing behind him.

Lucas smiled, though he had no idea why, his left cheek scraping the forest floor where he lay.

It considered him. Tall. Thick. Smelling of whiskey and sweat and sickness. It walked around to the front of him, and noticed he closed his eyes.

Over at the Dunlon place, folks said they heard a scream.

6

1892

"I'm not sure you should be here Mr. Stanton." It was Noel Flagler, the police officer. He looked pale, like he was sick, or about to be. His glossy, wavy yellow hair more wet than normal. Noel didn't wear a uniform or hat like the officers in Boston. Everyone in Sunbury knew he was the town's policeman.

Raymond knew Bill Kline, who was also there, standing next to Noel and rubbing the back of his neck, looking thoroughly uncomfortable. But he didn't know the other man, the old one who was crying in the small wooden stool next to Noel. Something on the old man's face made Raymond think he might be mentally unwell. Raymond was good with reading folks.

"I think it will be fine, Noel," said Josiah. "Raymond is a good man and a good friend. If we do have to form a party to search the woods, he may be a man we'd be best to take with us."

Noel didn't nod or give any sign that he agreed. Instead, he looked long and hard at Raymond and then down at the floor. Raymond had the sense Noel was angry at someone. But he also had the sense that Noel himself knew it wasn't at Raymond, who, after all, had merely come in here to speak with his friend, Dr. Hall.

"Raymond," Josiah said, "we have a situation, here."

Chapter 6

Raymond thought that that seemed about right, but he didn't say anything. He knew Josiah would get right to the point.

"This," he said gesturing only with his eyes, "is Hannibal Guthridge. His property is on the south side of town. What we have here is a murder. The victim," he said, without gesturing at all since it was obvious and Josiah was a spare talker, "is Ed Aimes." Sometimes all of a man's philosophy is brought to bear on the tense of a verb.

"What can I do to help?"

Raymond was asking both Noel and Josiah, but that wasn't immediately obvious. Josiah answered first.

"Could you come out with us on a search if Bill Kline stays here with Hannibal?"

Noel looked at Josiah, irritated at his presumption. But he wasn't irritated enough to revoke Dr. Hall's offer. Raymond Stanton stood nearly six feet and had broad shoulders and was a physically fit man. If whoever had stolen those bodies meant more trouble than whatever the act itself was supposed to mean, he would be a good man to have. And Bill Kline was capable enough of making sure Hannibal Guthridge didn't leave or stir up any more trouble than he already had.

Raymond watched Noel's face turn back to look at him and saw that he nodded. Then he asked, "Is this about the bodies I heard were dug up last night?"

Josiah didn't register any surprise that Raymond knew about it or go into any more detail. He merely nodded, and that was that.

The three of them left Bill and Hannibal in Josiah's office, since the building where the town's single cell was kept and where Noel had a wooden desk and chair that he used roughly once a week was on the north side of town, and none of them wanted to put off going back to the cemetery and getting the search for the bodies going.

"Care to share any suspicions you might have about what happened?"

Raymond was talking about the bodies, not about the murder, but oddly enough Josiah didn't need to ask. They were walking briskly down the last street before the dirt road that ran on the outer edge of town where the cemetery was. Out of the corner of his eye Josiah could see that Raymond had just the slightest edge of a smirk on his face. Ed Aimes' death wouldn't have caused that. Raymond was intrigued. Disturbed, but intrigued.

"Somebody carried them. Manually."

"How do you know?"

Josiah continued to walk with purpose, quickening his step as they came up over the small rise in the ground upon which the eastern edge of the cemetery lay. The dew was off the grass now, and the mid-summer sun was beginning to banish the shadows

Chapter 6

and the cool. Some of the men had hauled the dead horse away, which was good considering the society of flies and other wildlife it would have started to draw. The blood and some of its insides stretched from the spot between the graves in their direction, making the grass, flattened as it was by its body as they'd dragged it away with ropes, all the more conspicuous. Josiah thought about the fact that he didn't smell any fire or burning animal. He'd make sure before the end of the day that they did that. They didn't need a bear wandering into the village out of the woods, drawn by the carcass.

Raymond was startled by the blood and the sight of the dirt piled up on the west side of the two empty graves, but he didn't stop walking. He wanted to look inside the graves, though he didn't understand why. Down at the bottom of Mrs. Atwood's lay an open casket. The lid lay across the top at an angle, its top facing up correctly but looking as though it had been thrown down with little or no care. It was new wood, but the film of earth scattered across it and around it made it look hauntingly aged. Even though the sun was coming further up behind them, the shadows down in that hole, more than a man's height deep, left him with no impression that was normal. He felt sweat on his neck all of a sudden, and he had the thought that he was truly somehow a part of this.

Nephilim

"We will venture into the woods first," Noel said. "My hope is we'll find them with the help of Joe Mertz' dog. I don't claim to have any idea who desecrated these graves, but I believe out there is our best chance of finding them."

"I agree," said Josiah.

Raymond and Noel looked at him, surprised at the certainty in his voice. But no one said any more. Noel nodded, looked back over at Raymond once more, then waived Joe Mertz up to them as they stepped into the woods.

7

1843

What Marvin Branson knew about Sunbury's current circumstances he knew because June Bloomfield had told him. There had been a series of recent deaths, unexpected ones, and at least one disappearance. All of it taken together had put everyone June knew in a fearful and anxious state. More than a few people were wondering out loud whether a sickness or perhaps a cluster of calamities ordained by Providence were settling over Sunbury. And that simple bit of gossip had set Marvin to work down in the machinery of his mind. He continued to listen, and he had a slight smile under his finely trimmed black mustache that made older women like June think that he was a thoughtful and courteous young man, the kind of young man they would love for their daughters to marry. June had no daughters, only a young son, but she had plenty of that matronly song in her heart, and Marvin Branson persuaded her through that quiet smile and the melodic warmth in his voice and the little crystal quality in his eyes that he was just the sort of man she would love to see move to Sunbury and find a wife and perhaps be a Trustee someday.

At a quarter-past noon, Marvin Branson stepped quickly out of the Inn and stretched his neck just a bit, wrestling with the absurd tightness of his tie (the higher the stakes, the tighter he tied it) and took the information he'd recorded on a single sheet of paper to the eastern edge of town, where his secret was currently hidden, smoking a cigarette and reading a page of the Boston newspaper by oil lantern light in a barn that had been left vacant while the Glanville family was in St. Louis visiting relatives. That secret was named Theodore McCabe, and he smelled like brandy and paper currency and tobacco. He was on his back at the moment, his upper half resting against the door of an empty stall, and the shadows on his right side where the lantern's light didn't pierce struck Marvin as unflattering when he entered. Theodore looked dead, somehow, with only half of his face visible along with the fact that he didn't move even slightly when Marvin had entered the barn. And the sight of a dead man reading a newspaper was unsettling.

"How are you?"

It was a strange question. It was also a useless question, but Theodore chose to answer it, mostly out of sheer boredom.

"My left ear itches. I'm attempting to see how long I can go without scratching it. Also, there's a stray cat that slinks in through the open slat just behind you and to your left. It's hunting a mouse I suspect. Beyond those items, nothing interesting has happened to me in thirty-six hours."

Chapter 7

Marvin licked the inside of his upper lip. Theodore always made him uneasy because there was nothing that could be controlled about him. He was like a horse Marvin's uncle had once owned that he had seen, as a boy, the man try to ride any number of times. No matter what his uncle did, what he said, there was a will inside that horse that was impervious to his uncle's, to all the tricks he had learned to direct another living thing to his own ends. Marvin had learned over the past year that Theodore was useful, that he could help him make a great deal of money in the span of a week, sometimes even a single day, but that there was nothing he could do to truly direct Theodore's actions. He simply had to set up the opportunity and hope for the best. So far, he had always gotten it. At least when it counted.

"I'm sorry about our disconnect in Boston," Marvin said, with something like true remorse. It had the right cadence and head tilt to imitate remorse, anyway. But it didn't register with Theodore in the slightest. He closed his newspaper and stared at the barn wall just in front of him, considering something unknown to Marvin.

"You don't know anything about King Saul, do you?"

Marvin didn't answer, partly because he wasn't entirely sure he'd heard Theodore correctly, and partly because if he had, he had no earthly idea what it meant.

"Regret isn't something you can forge." Theodore was silent for a few seconds, then looked at Marvin and smiled theatrically, enough of an indication to Marvin that he could go on.

"I believe I have the play," Marvin said, grateful to get back to business. "There have been some very recent deaths here, untimely ones that have clearly left an impression on the residents. I'm confident that there's a general sense of disquiet among the people, and I think we'll be able to work our persuasions to great effect."

The act of verbal subterfuge, of putting what they did for money into vocabulary as innocuous as possible, was something Marvin had never noticed himself doing. But if he had been able to step outside of himself for a minute and see that he was standing in the pale light of a stranger's barn talking to a virtual stranger whose talents he had been using to devious ends for months but who also scared him, he would have seen something. Had Marvin observed himself a little more carefully, he might have seen that there was something odd about the fact that he acted guilty in this moment.

But he didn't, and so they worked out the plan quickly, knowing which steps could not be skipped and fully aware that if they were successful, Sunbury would be the location of their biggest score ever.

8

1892

It was quieter in the woods than Raymond had anticipated. There were no rustlings of squirrels, no birds chirping. Considering the warmth and relative clearness of the morning, that surprised him. He also noticed that he was breathing quickly. If Raymond had the observational skills of Dr. Hall, he would have noticed he was not the only one.

He began to count the steps between each sound of distant movement of any kind. Fourteen. Then six. Then twenty-one.

Did nothing live in these woods?

He didn't conjure it up willingly, but the thought of Laura Atwood's and David Steatham's lifeless forms being shuttled out into these woods seemed queerly not out of place now. It seemed as though only green things and wood breathed out here. He saw them as from above, from a place wedged within the thick treetops, as they were carried deeper into the woods by someone moving with strained but purposeful steps. It seemed real to him, and when he realized it was a daydream he was having, he broke it up and went back to counting steps in between sounds from anything other than their party.

They came upon Mrs. Atwood's shoes and necklace after twenty minutes of walking. The hound had shown some interest in the area, but Joe actually noticed them before the dog did. They were neatly placed at the foot of a young birch tree. No direct sunlight found them under the thick green blanket above their heads, just the scattered light that kept them from being in complete shadow. Though it was dim, Joe's eyes spotted them. He was the only woodsman among the men, having hunted regularly in the woods Sunbury was nested against and as a boy in Alberta. He had an eye for objects that didn't bear wild shape, and so he'd called out, and then a few seconds later his dog had run up to him and to the tree and sniffed around. The necklace was inside the shoes, left neatly as though it were meant to be found.

None of the men had said anything for a full minute, then Dr. Hall walked up to a brother birch a few yards further south. He rubbed his hand along the trunk slowly.

"Joe?"

Joe walked up to Dr. Hall and put his thick, wrinkled hands on his hips as he looked at the tree. When Raymond arrived on Josiah's left, he looked where their eyes appeared to be looking, but he couldn't make anything out.

All three men stared intently at the tree for a minute or so before Raymond admitted, "I don't know what we're looking at."

Chapter 8

"Buck marks," Joe said, as though that explained everything. Just then Raymond heard the soft earth and sparse grass rustle and crunch like wet newsprint behind him as Noel joined the three of them.

"Is that what I think it is?" Noel asked, nodding towards the tree.

"Yes," Josiah answered and knelt in front of the tree to take a closer look, though he was nearly certain he'd seen all he'd needed to.

"Why does it matter?" Noel asked.

"These are very much like the marks a male deer leaves on the trunk of a tree when it grinds its antlers against the bark," Josiah explained to Raymond, patiently and without even an ounce of dismissiveness. "The reason why it matters, Noel, is that these are new. The wood here that was under the bark is newly exposed." There was no trace of dismissiveness to Noel, either. "I've not seen instances of bucks marking trees in summer. Spring and fall both, but never summer."

Joe stuck his thick tongue down in between his big lower lip and his bottom teeth in thought before agreeing. "I can't say I have either. Not even once." He rubbed his cheeks. "How's it...?" He nodded towards the most obvious problem with the idea that they were buck marks, though, and Dr. Hall raised his left eyebrow in response.

"I don't know exactly what this means," Dr. Hall eventually said, "but I think the odds are against us finding two unrelated and unlikely phenomena so close together. Either they aren't unlikely or are they aren't unrelated. And I think we'd all agree they are definitely *unlikely*."

All four men stood under the shadows of the sheets of leaves two dozen feet above their heads and thought about what that meant. Somehow the dead woman's shoes and necklace being neatly placed right here in these woods and this good-sized scraping pattern on the trunk of a birch tree were related.

"Whoever stole those bodies hacked away at this tree?" Joe asked as his dog sniffed the earth all around them inquisitively.

"I don't see a blade doing this," Josiah said without even looking back at the tree. "Anything as sharp as a knife or an ax would have left more distinct marks, instead of what this appears to be, shaving the bark off gradually through rubbing, like bucks do."

"Somebody rubbed this tree?" Noel sounded both irritable and incredulous. He'd already reached the same conclusion as Josiah. He just had no idea what it meant. Which left him only a half-step behind.

"Bucks rub trees with their antlers to mark their territory and to scrape off the film that covers new antler growth." Josiah looked from Noel back to Raymond, though Raymond had no idea why. He knew

Chapter 8

it was intentional. He could tell it from the slight raise in Josiah's right eyebrow, but he couldn't discern what Josiah meant in looking to him at that particular moment.

"Until some other evidence persuades me otherwise, I think that whoever or whatever stole Mrs. Atwood's and Mr. Cheatham's bodies and killed Mr. Guthridge's horse did to this tree what bucks do to trees."

"The mark's seven feet up," said Joe.

"Yes," said Josiah, raising both eyebrows at Raymond. "It is."

* * *

Rachel had refreshed herself with some cold water applied to her face with her own hands. She trembled a bit as she kept them there over her eyes, hovering over the basin and staring into the blackness and working to change the course of her thoughts.

The hens. That was the next thing she needed to do, and she needed her wits and her arms and her legs to cooperate in order to do it. She wiped her brow with the white sleeve of her blouse and took a breath so deep it made her cough, after which she laughed at herself. She then straightened her dress and made her way quickly outside.

Nephilim

They owned four hens, from which they had received a grand total of three eggs thus far. Her father was good-natured enough about it, giving a silent smile to Rachel every time she came in the back door of the house frustrated that another day had come and gone without an egg to show for their efforts. Rachel was determined to make the experiment work, especially in light of the fact that purchasing the hens had been her idea.

The ordinary expenses of life were met by Raymond's estate; his father had been a wealthy businessman in Baltimore. But they lived meagerly by design, and Raymond had instilled in his children, as he had in himself, the conviction that they should work hard to provide for themselves as much as possible. The eggs had been a contribution Rachel had hoped to make.

The sun was high enough in the sky by now that there were no shadows behind the house, and Rachel felt the heat on the back of her neck as she made her way to the coop. It was shingled because Raymond had decided to throw himself into the project as much as time would allow. At the front was the small door with a tiny pin lock that he had devised over an entire Saturday three weeks prior. As Rachel squatted and opened the little hen-sized door and squinted into the darkness, she noticed the etching on the birch tree a few yards away on the western edge of their property.

Chapter 8

It was scratched into the trunk of the tree very deeply, as though it had been carved by an angry hand. She stood up without remembering to shut the door of the coop, and she felt her heart flutter as she took the seventeen steps up to the tree. The back of her neck felt cold suddenly.

The etching was very much like something a child would draw, though much higher than any child could reach without help. There were no low branches that would have done for climbing.

The pale gray of the bark and its brown flesh underneath peeking out through strips of open places suddenly impressed upon her the image of an old man's hands. And that it made worse.

There was something unnatural in the image, as though it were tilted against the level of the world, but only just enough to make her feel wobbly as she looked at it.

The carving was of a woman. Rachel knew that only because of the two lines on either side of the oval head, lines that curved away from the head and that seemed to be long, feminine hair, and from similar lines around the body that she was certain were intended to represent a dress. But the woman's head was so bent down that it was lower than where her left shoulder would have been. Beneath the woman were what looked like waves, carved intentionally to be at different heights, as though a symbol for water wasn't what was meant so much as some sort of representation of actual waves in an actual ocean.

She wanted to look behind her, as though whoever had carved this during the night was still there, but she found herself unable to move anything but her right hand, which was scratching her left elbow so hard that it drew blood through the sleeve of her blouse. She felt a buzzing in her ears.

It looked like something a little boy would draw after a nightmare, though not so much from residual fear as from rage. But Rachel had an inexplicable and yet undeniable certainty that it was not a child who had done it.

She heard two of the hens behind her and finally regained control of her body and turned around. She blinked fiercely three times in an effort to clear the fear away and studied the two white hens as they walked in opposite directions, the one on her right flapping its wings a few times as it strutted across the grass.

Perhaps she would ask her father about it when he returned. For now, she would feed the hens. The sun was bright, and that was a good thing.

* * *

Three more hours in the woods led to nothing, and all four men were discouraged. Dr. Hall was most frustrated, though he wore it differently than the others.

Chapter 8

He had expected that the dog would be able to find the bodies after they had so quickly found Mrs. Atwood's shoes and necklace. He had no explanation for why there was nothing else, no article of clothing, no foreign object dropped by the thief, nothing at all anywhere within a half-mile of that spot. And he was certain he *should* have an explanation.

Josiah Hall was more ready to accommodate than the other three men the possibility that whatever had dug up and stolen the bodies and had killed Hannibal Guthridge's horse wasn't a man. He knew he was out of step with them in this, and so he didn't pursue the issue any further until he and Raymond were alone, back in his office that evening.

Ed Aimes' body had been taken to Joel Fremont, the undertaker (whose bald head and pale skin made him look very much, at least to Raymond's eyes, like what an undertaker could be expected to resemble), and Raymond had made a trip home to Rachel to deliver her dress and to tell her he would not be eating supper tonight and, with some discretion, why.

Now, under the oil lamp on Dr. Hall's desk and what was left of the day's sun, Josiah decided to let his thoughts stretch their legs in the presence of his friend. Raymond and he were kindred hearts.

Raymond waited for Josiah to speak first, now that both were seated, and the only sound was the subtle, mechanical ticking of the small wooden clock at the corner of Josiah's desk, just under the windowsill.

"Will you tell me what you think?"

He expected Josiah to smile, like a man who knew too well the hand of poker he was playing, like the strength of that hand was enough to lift his lips and his eyes and his spirit. But Josiah didn't smile. He stared at Raymond but didn't think of him, his eyes there, but his mind engaged in something else, despite the fact that he'd heard him. He had the barrel of a fountain pen in his mouth, the nib of it resting in between his left index finger and thumb while the other end was between his front teeth, and Raymond knew that whatever Josiah said would be right. He was the most intelligent man Raymond had ever met, and the least impulsive, and those two qualities taken together would mean he'd be as likely to be correct as anyone.

"This has happened before."

It was among the things Raymond least expected to hear, and like most unexpected sentences Raymond's mind had trouble attaching meaning to the words. By the time Josiah had pulled an old, red, clothbound book off of his desk and opened it to the page he'd intended, the fourth page, Raymond understood the bare meaning. What he did not understand was how the stealing of bodies from graves accompanied by slaughtering of horses had happened before in Sunbury. That seemed unlikely even to a well-traveled mind.

Chapter 8

Josiah began reading from the book.

"Accompanied Joseph Carlysle to the proposed site of his new facility, Jessup Creek having already been established as a suitable water source, our surveyor, Mr. Edward Hall, made note of the lines of the proposed property purchase from the village, but in doing so recognized a terrible stench on the southwest edge of said proposed purchase. It was a heavily wooded area with the creek nowhere near, and so such an overpowering odor seemed difficult to account for. After an hour's exploration we discovered a small cave of limestone hidden to us until we came around to it from the south. A high limestone hill covered entirely in small trees and hearty topsoil had been split ages ago through erosion or some other force, and the crack was quite large enough for a man, or even two with care if the men not too large, as none of us were, to step into and explore in its entirety. We determined the depth of the cave to be no more than thirty feet, but this was only with great determination to make a measurement after discovering the source of the odor, which was the foulest and most debilitating I have ever experienced.

"At the very back of this low, narrow cavern were perhaps ten or twenty masses of former life, all in various states of decomposition. Using a lantern for light, we were able to determine that none were human, but that nearly all were intact. Upon realizing what we had stumbled into, the hibernating place of some large and capable predator, we quickly conferred with Trustees Williamson and Davenport and deputized a squadron of viable young men to locate and dispose of this creature. Mr. Carlysle having considerable confidence in the decisive action of our town, his purchase has been finalized as of this Monday prior, January the 14th, 1841."

Josiah closed the book for a moment and looked out his window, sitting directly above his desk and facing Beadle Street. It was nearly night, now, and the movement of the flame in the lantern twisted his own reflection in the glass as though it were a pool he were peering into, disturbed by the sudden movement of some dark creature. Raymond thought, for the first time, that Josiah looked like an old man, despite the fact that he was not in point of fact an old man yet. But his strained eyes had what a less knowledgeable soul might mistake for cynicism. It was actually measured hope and strength. Josiah Hall knew what he was and what he could do and could not. In that regard alone, he was very much what Sunbury needed.

"There's more."

Raymond said it knowing Josiah well enough, despite the fact that it had only been nineteen days since the first time they'd shared a meal together, to know that a direct connection existed between the past and what had happened last night. Josiah was not one to overstate his thoughts. He was right.

Chapter 8

Josiah nodded. He pulled a black leather case off the right side of his desk and opened it. Inside was a collection of what looked to Raymond to be fifty or so sheets of personal stationary, yellowed with several decades of passed time, but crisp and with the black strokes of good ink still very legible.

"These are personal notes from Sidney Seagram's desk as Trustee," Josiah said. "He served from 1837 to 1846. He was also founder and president of Sunbury Bank. I acquired them from his son Matthias, before he left to settle somewhere in western Pennsylvania."

Josiah didn't look up at Raymond at all, his eyes were fixed on something in the corner of the office, just behind Raymond and to the right, but Raymond didn't feel the need to see what it was. Then his friend looked back down at the old paper and read.

"I regret my deceit in the matter of JC's acquisition. I have as of yet not seen the full scope of that deceit, but it is to my great regret that I believe it will be no insignificant one. While at the time I appeared to be able to justify it to myself as a matter more engaged in for the good of the village and the people of our area than one in which I would personally benefit, I now see that no one man can know all the ill effects of his lie at the time. We are told to tell the truth by Providence because only Providence knows the end of a matter from the beginning. Our lies may be the germ of some greater demise, as I fear will be the case here.

"There were fourteen human forms in the cave that we discovered at the southwest edge of JC's proposed property. We did not permit the surveyor to join us in the cave, and we made no disclosure to him about the true nature of our discovery. JC and I wanted to better understand the situation presented to us, and with clearer heads we nervously returned to the site the following day. We brought along PB, taken into our confidence, and with his knowledge of the woods and the local geography taken together with my own, we were able to determine the location from which these remains had been absconded. The cholera hospital several miles away from our village which ceased its operations a little over a year ago had maintained its own preserve for the placement of its patients who expire, and we were, with some effort, able to recreate the trek from that cemetery, such as it is, to the cave in JC's proposed site. It was indescribably distressing to come to such a disturbance, heaps of earth and holes in the ground where there had once been a final repository of the remains of living souls. It was no tremendous feat to confirm that the bodies in the cave had been taken from that place, though no purpose or agent of the theft could be discerned.

"Inasmuch as the greater good appeared to be in proceeding with the establishment of JC's mill, we

Chapter 8

agreed to quietly arrange for the return of the remains and to make no further inquiries into the matter. While I do not know all that may proceed from what I've done, I do fear that it will end darkly."

Josiah closed the cloth book and set it on his desk and looked Raymond in the eye for the first time. Before he could say what he intended, Raymond spoke.

"That was over fifty years ago," Raymond said, his voice firm and yet knowing in the corners of his mind Josiah would convince him of the truth of whatever conclusion he'd reached. "No one man who was inexplicably stealing corpses from a cholera graveyard would still be in a position to be doing it now."

"I don't believe a man was doing it then or now." Josiah said it the way Raymond imagined a carpenter would describe the shape of the next cut he was making in the wood before him. Josiah's voice was precise and carried just the barest sense of his design under them, the voice of a workman.

"You don't?" Raymond didn't intend his smile to be sardonic, or rather didn't intend to reveal that it was. But it was. Raymond was incredulous, not because he immediately ruled out some such possibility, but because it struck him as discordant to the fact that he was sitting in a doctor's office wearing trousers he'd purchased in Philadelphia and under the light of an oil lamp nearly identical to the one sitting in his bedroom at home. His setting felt far too normal for something unknown to his senses to have entered the conversation.

"A devil? A vampire? What sort of creature, then?"

Josiah excused the half-smile on his friend's face, determined actually to pay it no mind at all.

"Our view of the world is too small because our view of the God who made it is too small. Most of the studied Christians I've met who don't believe there were once giants don't disbelieve it because of a textual consideration, but because they don't believe God can make and put down giants. Tell me you don't believe Goliath was as tall as this ceiling here because of something written in our Bibles and I'll walk with you. But try to make it not be in your Bible and I'll simply know you don't believe our Maker is listening to our conversation, or that He split the ground to swallow Korah and his friends, or that He once doused this whole world in cold water deeper than the mountains. The world is a much more frighteningly real place than most of our preachers give it credit for, and that's because the God they preach is a much more frighteningly real God than they give Him credit for. I believe in giants, whatever they were, because I believe Him."

Raymond's mouth was dry, and his neck and arms were tingling. "Josiah, are you actually saying there's a

Chapter 8

giant in those woods? And that it's what stole those bodies and gutted that horse?" It was telling that Raymond's first emotion was excitement, and a sense that had he found they were even more blood brothers than he'd thought at suppertime today, not one of skepticism, as Noel's or Joe's would have been.

"No, not with certainty. But I am saying that the few facts I have taken together indicate to me we are not dealing with a typical human man, and that I am open to the possibility that there are still things with beating hearts on this earth that are not typical human men."

Raymond turned the words over in his mind, bearing with them the facts as he knew them himself. He was no theologian, no investigative authority, and no medical man. And yet he found he was more confident in Josiah's conclusion than he would have expected.

"I agree with you."

Josiah Hall nodded his head and smiled, but he regretted that he'd done so. Then and later.

9

1843

The first session was at the Inn, and that was by design. Marvin knew from experience and intuition that the more familiar he was with the setting the more he could control. He had seen firsthand that afternoon in the tavern and in conversation outside the general store that the several fever fatalities along with a few other tragic events in recent weeks had worked sufficient effects in Sunbury for the ground to be very fertile for him. There were nine people who gathered in the front room of Harold Bloomfield's house, what Marvin had taken to calling the "parlor" to the individuals he had persuaded to attend the event.

"In speaking across the divide, chancing what is perhaps the most tenuous and dangerous of connections available to us as men and women of flesh and blood, it is necessary that we prepare our own minds for what may transpire. It can be unsettling."

This was, with two word changes, the opening he had used six consecutive times now, stretching back almost four months. The inflection on the nouns, *divide*, *connections*, *flesh*, *blood*, needed just the right breath of seriousness and fear on the part of the speaker, enough to create the mood the event required but not so much as to arouse suspicion.

Chapter 9

He did not believe he had a problem in this group of individuals. Each was chosen for that particular reason. These would, of course, be his human advertisements for what he hoped would be as many as five profitable events in Sunbury. But he had also learned, in two prior cases, that an apparently gullible man or woman may actually see through the theatrics and bring the whole enterprise to a crashing halt. The last time it happened a man named Frank with cracked hands and blackened fingernails had grunted halfway through Theodore's shaking of the trick bureau and then quietly explained to his aunt Anna that he had seen a better version of this particular trick in a theater in St. Louis. It had surprised Marvin as he was so sure the man had been an imbecile prepared to believe whatever he would offer by way of illusion, that he found himself stuttering out a few words and then standing frozen and stock still so long that he eventually had to excuse himself, ask that the curtains be drawn and the whole operation be suspended for lack of belief (a strange twist of irony that escaped Marvin) and returned the money to his clearly agitated hostess as he clumsily and angrily collected the materials and hauled them out the door.

Every muscle in Marvin's face was a tool, a utility used to communicate what he wanted communicated. He bit his own lower lip to indicate even he, the experienced and trustworthy guide into this shadowy world, was nervous. He flared his nostrils as he drew in a deep breath so that everyone could see he indeed prepared for what he knew would be momentous. He arched one black eyebrow as he began to hum the single note that opened the proceedings, that single raised eyebrow a subtle sign of confidence now that the familiar door was being opened. Marvin Branson was a remarkably effective pitchman, a man of the highest skill in the art of selling false goods to true people. He knew what would earn trust, and he knew what people wanted, and as he was in a position to provide something that had the appearance of that desired product, he was now a reasonably wealthy man as well.

Theodore played his part perfectly. The table rattled when it was supposed to, the bureau door flew open just as the lantern's light went out, and the empty chair fell over with great result. Marvin was even able to shed a surprised tear at the revelation that *that* was June Bloomfield's deceased mother's favorite type of flower, the one he had spoken aloud with closed eyes and pained face during his period of connection.

Marvin's excitement at the fertile soil of Sunbury's good people, his assurances that this indeed was clearly a season of great opportunity for messages to be sent and received to loved ones now passed, was as a match on dry kindling. All nine people promised they would be bringing dear friends to his event tomorrow night. Marvin had clearly been sent to them

Chapter 9

to do this work in a time of great need. And Marvin himself was delighted and clearly moved at their happiness and the benefit he was able to be to them. Harold Bloomfield thought to himself that Marvin Branson was a singularly honest, capable man. A man of the highest quality. He insisted on giving him twelve dollars extra from his own savings as a gesture of generosity.

10

1892

Noel took off his hat just inside the door of his house. He could smell biscuits, and that cheered him a bit, but not enough to show on his face. He stood there in the dim light of the hall that led past the sitting room to the kitchen and dining room. The lantern in the kitchen cast enough steady light into the hall that he could see his hands, the dirt from the woods still caked on his right and the left one shaking at the thumb and index finger. He bit his lower lip and wondered if there was something haunted, something unnatural stealing bodies and killing horses and living out there in those woods, just a half-mile west of his house. The house where his wife and two sons slept. The house where he could smell biscuits and hear Patricia humming and the boys playing.

After half a minute he decided there was nothing to be done about it right there in the hall, and that thinking about it any longer wouldn't help to get anything done. He would go into the kitchen and say good evening and wash the dirt from off his hands. The wood floors creaked under his shoes as he made his way into the house, and when he passed into the open kitchen and dining room Patricia looked up at him without smiling but still with warmth. She was intent on finishing the dinner preparations. He nodded politely

Chapter 10

before her eyes went back down to what she was doing, then he looked down at Stephen and Lawrence, his two blond-headed boys, who were playing with a small toad in a box that they had between them.

"Good evening, Daddy," they said, more or less at the same time and with the same affection. Noel smiled at them and then went to collect water to rinse the soil and the residue of moss from his hands, and as he did so he heard something very much like a howl, small and shrill and sharp, a note of ice in his ears. He knew immediately that it was not anyone in the village.

* * *

Rachel heard it, too, from where she was seated in the front room of the house, a copy of *The Pilgrim's Progress* on her lap, her eyes having run over the same sentence six times. A last strand of steam from her cooling tea dissipated into the air of the room, and then it was just clear air and the yellow-orange light of the lamp on her right. The sound was a flat note on the moment of normal summer evening sounds, the comforting, subtle click of the flame and the crickets chirping by the thousands in the still lush grass and the owl that lived in the oak tree at the back of their property. It was no normal animal. She knew that from the first. It rose towards the end of the note it sounded, the call or scream or howl, and in that rise, it almost sounded like a laugh given in great pain or insanity. It was intelligent, she knew that, and she wondered for a moment what sort of a drunk would be out that direction, out towards the woods where there were no houses and only the bare dirt road and the cemetery. Then she remembered what had happened this morning, the little she had heard from her father and the more she had heard from Mrs. Tufts when she'd gone into the village herself.

Rachel closed the book and stood up, and before she knew it, she'd opened the door and stepped out into the small yard they kept in the front of their house. Across the road was Miles and Joan Cartwright's house, and neither had come out themselves to see what the sound was. For several seconds, Rachel wondered if she might have imagined the howl, since otherwise someone else would have heard it and almost certainly come out to see. But she dismissed that thought and made her way around the house and into the back, looking out over their property and into the deep black night that lay over the flat land and beyond that the cemetery and beyond that the woods.

The dark was untouched by any lanterns from any other houses in that direction. Only one or two homes lay between them and the cemetery and the woods due west. But there was enough moonlight for her to be able make out the rise of the ground at the cemetery, and she thought she could even form in her mind the outlines of the unbroken miles of forest that began at

Chapter 10

the eastern edge of the cemetery. She was surprised to find herself walking into the darkness without any hesitation. Whatever the sound had been, it had been unordinary, and it had been nearer their home than she might have liked, and her first instinct was to get closer to where it had come from and see if she might hear it again.

For a brief moment she heard the rustling of air and a sound like the crinkling of old, thin paper, then the world swam around her in a disorienting circle as she fell to the ground. She didn't realize she'd been hit and toppled over by something until almost a minute had gone by. What startled her out of the dreamy sensation that had overcome her was the scream of a woman somewhere behind her, and at that point she recognized the metallic taste of blood in her mouth, and the pain at the back of her head and in her left arm. She stuttered out a cry of her own, but it came out half-formed and hoarse, and she knew before trying again that her father was not here and there was no one else out of doors to help her. She twisted herself enough to confirm that the Cartwright's door was still shut, then used her right arm to push herself into a sitting position. She did not know for sure what a fracture felt like, but she was fairly certain she had one in her other arm. The pain was sharp and debilitating, like a blinding, charging, fire that sprang up from her left hand into her brain and then back again. She thought she might regurgitate, but with the passage of a few more seconds she determined she could control her stomach and was able, with one horrifying near tumble, to stand up and look off in the direction, away from the woods and toward the village, of the scream she'd just heard.

The Cartwright's front door opened, facing her, and Miles Cartwright calmly but with apparent curiosity stepped out into the dark evening and planted his booted feet into the sod of the wedge of his property that came up to the road. He worked his tongue against the left side of his jaw and stared at the village, a half-mile or so behind his home, and then came back to his door. Rachel presumed he was going back inside to grab his rifle or to get his oldest son, Timothy, and her heart sunk as she realized she couldn't cry out. Her mouth still felt slippery with the moistness that came from her stomach sickness, and her throat seemed to be in another body in another town far away. She needed Miles to look over and see her, to bring her inside and let her wait until her father came home, but he was already inside his own front door now, though the door was open and let out a flickering orange glow against the night surrounding it.

Rachel knew that whatever had knocked her down might still be here in the night around her, and she also knew that she would not be able to see it from where she was now. There was only the moonlight

Chapter 10

above and Miles Cartwright's front door's orange glimmer, and with that light she could barely see her own feet.

There were no more screams from the village. A moment later Miles and Timothy and his next son, whose name Rachel couldn't remember, stepped out their front door and walked around the south side of their home and faced the village. After a moment's hesitation, Miles began to lead Timothy towards town. But before Rachel could cry, the son whose name she couldn't remember looked in the direction of the Stanton property and saw Rachel, with dirt blackening the left side of her face and holding her left arm with her right hand, and called out to his father and brother that Mr. Stanton's daughter was hurt.

* * *

Raymond and Josiah were walking across Beadle Street when they heard a woman's scream just south of the village. Without saying anything to each other they began walking in the direction of the scream intently. By the time they realized that that was what each of them was doing, they were within sight of Lucas Meyers' home, where his wife Hannah was standing outside with her back against the western wall of their cabin. She was crying with her eyes closed, and Raymond noticed that her clenched right hand was shaking. He could make it out even from a distance because of the lamps still on in the Meyers' home streaming out through their open door and the lamps on in the homes of their two direct neighbors, both of whom had their own front doors open. His heart felt strangely charged and sick at the same time, and he sensed a heaviness in his tongue as well. Something about what he was seeing and had just heard felt like a memory, but not one that he could name. Rose's face was present in his mind as they came up to the front of the house, even though Hannah Meyers looked nothing like Rose.

"Can we be of help, Lucas?" Josiah asked as Lucas Meyers came back around the house from the rear, holding a long rifle by the barrel in his left hand. He looked sharp and angry. Lucas was a tall man with thinning yellow-brown hair and a thick mustache, and his face was red in the light and in his anger. Raymond looked at the rifle in his hand uneasily for a second, but then looked back at Hannah, and asked Lucas, "Is everything all right?"

"No, it is not! Something just came tearing through my property and frightened my wife nearly to death. She said-" He paused and looked back into the shadows behind the house, then turned back to look back at both of them, first Josiah and then Raymond. "She said it was large. And unnaturally quick." He pursed his lips and breathed long and hard out of his

Chapter 10

nose, then arched his back and turned again, without saying a word, to walk back into the darkness.

Raymond and Josiah followed him, stepping out of the glow of the doors of the Meyers' and their neighbors' homes and into the thick darkness of a night with half a moon. Neither Josiah nor Raymond had a rifle or any weapon, but neither gave it much thought as they walked a few paces behind Lucas and listened for whatever sound the man or the creature might make.

Raymond expected something, a ruffle of the grass as it shifted or ran again further out in the shadow or another scream at one of the other houses nearby or perhaps breathing or snorting of whatever or whoever it was. But the only sounds were inside the houses behind them, and their own footsteps on the tall summer grass. Raymond was surprised, and something about the music of a normal summer night accompanied only by the breathing of the other two men seemed out of place to him, fragile in a night this hostile. He knew this thing, or man, had something to do with the dead horse, and probably, as hard as it was for him to understand, the stolen bodies. Things like this just didn't happen in Sunbury; he knew that much despite his short residency in the village. To be in the middle of a night where a drunken fiend or a crazed grave robber or something less imaginable to him presently was back in the heart of the village and seeking to do harm to women like Mrs. Meyers all while the normal sounds and scents of summer revolved around them was unsettling. It was like looking at a painting by a sick and deranged and violent man, a painting of normal and beautiful things, but with the incongruities that would come from the falsehood of such a man trying to ape good and proper beauty. The smiles on the people would be disquieting and unreal, the flowers would be disproportionately large, because the man had never admired the beauty of a flower, the sky would be too blue and the sun too perfectly placed and colored and sized to be the real sun. This night was too much like a happy summer night; he heard crickets chirping all around him, now, and the smell of tall, seeding grass was so pleasant it was appetizing. Mrs. Meyers had just seen, or almost seen, someone or something evil that meant to do violence to the people of the village; this night had no business being pleasant.

All three men heard it at the same time. They had stepped into the shadows in a southerly direction about fifty yards when they discerned the low branches on a grove of young trees a stone's throw further south of them rustling all at once, loudly and violently, as though a bull had run through them. Lucas Meyers had raised his rifle and given a soft "shh" before Raymond and Josiah had given much thought to what it meant and before they had placed the sound exactly. Lucas knew this field just south of his property and a half-mile or so from the northern edge of the woods, and he knew

Chapter 10

what coyotes sounded like when they ran. He wouldn't have raised his rifle for a coyote.

All three men advanced slowly and cautiously, not wanting to make any noises that might cause whoever or whatever it was to run or charge. After six steps, Raymond heard the unmistakable sound of a single, long breath. He pictured it as an exhale, though it would have been hard for him to identify that it was because the volume decreased towards the end. But he was right. None of them moved when immediately after the breath came the sound of hard, fast beatings on the ground beneath the tall grass. Josiah shouted just before all three of them were toppled. In a few seconds, Lucas Meyers was standing again and aiming his rifle at where he thought the man was. But Raymond was still on the ground, with moving white sparks sliding to the right in his field of vision. He was terribly dizzy, and he couldn't orient which way he was laying on the ground or where Josiah and Lucas were. He rolled onto his back quickly, not wanting whatever had knocked him over to have a chance of being behind him.

Lucas shouted angrily into the night, but was careful not to fire. He had made several kills of violent creatures at night before, and in principle he was prepared for killing or capturing whatever had frightened his wife and bowled the three of them over. But he was nervous, thinking for the first time that it was possibly a bear.

Raymond heard another single shout from Josiah, and then the alarming sound of grass being rustled in the invisible field to his right, and the rustling sound drifting lower suddenly along with the thudding of what had to be feet beside it. Instinctively, Raymond understood that his friend was being dragged away, dragged in a southerly direction and quickly. Less instinctively he jumped to his feet and ran in the same direction. He shouted "Stop!" at the top of his lungs, then hit an exposed root of a single old maple tree and found himself face down in the bare dirt under its canopy.

The thudding and rustling had stopped. He heard Josiah groan a few yards in front of him, then he heard shorter grass rustling as whatever had been dragging Josiah turned and began to walk back towards Raymond.

The feeling that gripped his heart was one of a peculiarly dangerous but yet frightened evil. He had no idea what birthed that sense, or what made it so overpowering that he stopped breathing, nor did he have any time to consider it. He knew what was walking back toward him was wicked and also confused, much as he imagined an injured wild beast would be. But he knew from the steadiness of the steps that it was no beast. Whether a man or something worse, the creature could *think*. It had turned around slowly, gingerly when Raymond had tripped, and now was walking back with

Chapter 10

the caution and precision of a man. It was not sniffing the ground or sprinting at another potential meal the way a mere animal would. It was looking through the darkness at Raymond, considering, wondering, weighing.

Raymond couldn't see anything, and the fear and revulsion at the feeling of its evil would have made it difficult for him to roll over and think clearly even if he could. But he knew it had arrived at the spot just to the right of his head by the smell, something like wet, rotted wood, and by the fact that the noise of its steps had ceased. He tried to roll over, but he felt something hard press into his back and keep him pressed against the earth and the other roots of the old tree that were just above the ground's surface. He grimaced from the pain as it changed the shape of his spine and his ribs constricted under its weight and were pressed into the wood of one of the roots, but he made no sound. Then he heard the unmistakable boom of a rifle shot, and the pressing in his back stopped immediately, and he heard the quick sound of the footsteps running south again, away towards the end of the village and the woods. He pushed himself up with his hands, and before he had any time to consider it, he was running in the same direction as fast as he could.

The sound of two feet a dozen yards or so in front of him was getting harder to hear as his own heartbeat faster and faster. He realized he wasn't getting any closer to the man or creature. Despite a visceral fear of striking something else in the silent, invisible grass beneath him and tripping again, he quickened his pace and squinted into the thick darkness, looking for the shape of what he was chasing.

He was able to make out the horizon of the woods coming up in the distance, the tops of the trees blacking out the stars. He couldn't see the thing in front of him, but he could still hear its two feet, he was sure it was two feet, thumping against the ground not terribly far ahead. Despite the overpowering burning in his lungs and his legs he was able to consider that he had not heard Lucas behind him. He assumed he must have stayed with Josiah. It gave him a spark of simple fear to know that if he caught up with the being, he would be totally alone. He could not quite place himself in relation to the village in this darkness, but without looking back he imagined the southernmost house before the wild fields led up to the edge of the ocean of woods was at least a quarter of a mile behind him.

He reached the woods rather suddenly and realized that he did not hear any footfalls anymore. He slowed his steps as he came under the first few trees and was surprised at the difference the moon being covered made in his ability to see, and at the difference in smell under the trees. There was a smell of activity, of closeness and green life, of leaves and vines and wood and dead plants and moist wood. He wondered

Chapter 10

how close he was to whatever it was, and came to a stop, putting his hand on the faintest outline of a tree in front of him as he drew in and let out deep breaths. Suddenly he heard the sound of an owl not far away and jumped back a bit. As he did his left arm brushed against something much too soft and malleable to be a tree. The sound of running resumed, and he realized he had just touched the thing, and turned his face left to see if he could make it out or perhaps even follow it again. But it was far too dark to see anything more than a few feet away. He put his hands on his knees, lowered his head, and waited for his heart to slow.

11

1843

Marvin's anticipation for the second gathering had steadily increased throughout the day. June Bloomfield had clasped his hand that morning and said she simply had to convey something to him. As she poured out a cataract of words on the suspicions of her friends and neighbors that some spiritual terror had come to afflict Sunbury and had now made its presence known, he saw in her forehead and her eyes and her mannerisms that he was incredibly fortunate. Here would be fifteen, twenty, maybe more, all people ready to provide as much remuneration as he would humbly request in return for his dutiful and pained services as a contact with the darkness and light of the other side. He could talk to the dead, send messages to them, and perhaps given enough time and thought and energy could even see the minds and purposes of the demonic shadow who no doubt was causing mischief, even harm, in Sunbury's midst.

Of course he could do no such thing. But charlatans exist in every age and every country. Marvin was the sort who ran mechanically, like a clock. He did not care if people did go on to anywhere after their hearts stopped beating and their lungs ceased breathing, or at least he didn't care whether anyone else did, and he had almost no consideration as to whether he would

Chapter 11

when the distant event finally occurred to him. He simply had cravings, and money was the steady object of those cravings, and this was the easiest way he had stumbled upon of obtaining it. At least it was the easiest one which would not greatly interfere with his love of ease and long hours of sleep.

His companion, Theodore, was a different man with a different kind of heart. He made Marvin uneasy, though Marvin did his best to not consider the fact. He viewed Theodore's strangeness, the oddity in his look that made him seem ready to dissect you, perhaps literally, as something best left alone, out of sight, away from thought.

Marvin was drinking a whiskey at a table in the corner of the tavern on Beadle Street at one o'clock in the afternoon and watching the bartender read the paper. In his mind, he was considering what having three times as much money as he'd ever had to deposit in his account in Boston would feel like, what the sensation of electricity in his hand might be as he wrote the numbers on the slip of paper that he would hand to the bespectacled clerk and enjoyed the moment of elation and satisfaction. But as he played it through in his mind for the fifth time, his heart suddenly pounded several uncomfortable beats in succession, and he felt the room get colder. Theodore walked into the tavern, looked around at the empty tables in the middle of the room, spotted Marvin in the back corner, then walked up to the bar itself and told the man what he'd have. Marvin couldn't hear it from where he was, but the man poured something from a green bottle into a small glass like Marvin's. Vermouth, perhaps. Or Rum.

Marvin realized his upper lip was sweating and trembling. Theodore hadn't looked back at him since sitting down at the bar. He was talking with the bartender politely about something, and as Marvin looked down so as to not draw attention to the fact that they knew each other, he leaned in a bit towards the two of them in the hopes that he might pick up any strips of their dialogue. He made as though he were fixing something on his left boot and leaned out so far that he almost fell over, but he wasn't able to interpret a word of what they were saying. He sat back in his chair and downed the rest of his whiskey, and then, despite his best intentions, he looked back up at the two of them. He did it just in time to see Theodore gesture over to him and the bartender look where Theodore was pointing. Theodore looked right into Marvin's eyes and nodded, then raised his right eyebrow and said something else imperceptible to the bartender.

The fear Marvin felt was very much like a man who has been caught with his mistress by a wife whom he would very much like to keep. There was a great deal at stake here in Sunbury, and the only one who could expose the nature of the services Marvin provided was sitting there sipping rum and telling the bartender

Chapter 11

something that might destroy them both. For perhaps the fortieth time since the two had begun working together Marvin wondered what it was that Theodore wanted in life, what drove him to do anything, up to and including pretending to be the deceased in Marvin Branson's lucrative traveling hypocrisy practice.

He had just resolved to simply go up and introduce himself to Theodore and talk with him under the guise of noticing he had gestured to him and asking if they might have perhaps met on a train before. But just as he felt the tingle in his left hand that was the signal he was about to take the leap, Theodore stood and began to walk the twenty or so feet across the large room to Marvin's table. The room looked blurry to Marvin for a moment. He thought he might be dying but decided all he could do was continue to keep his posture as best he could and try to get Theodore to quietly tell him what he was up to. He briefly considered murdering the man, but had no idea how to commit and get away with murder, and the activity would carry with it far too many risks, far more than he was comfortable with. Comfort was something Marvin prized above all. He curled his toes up in his boots as Theodore closed the last several feet, and he gave himself the pleasure of imagining Theodore begging for his life as he prepared to dispatch him with an axe. He couldn't help smiling at that, indiscreet as smiling right now was.

"Hello."

That was it. The simple word spoken from a smirking face. A face with a frustratingly brown mustache, brown the color of dead wood, brown that reminded Marvin of wet dirt clinging to his trousers and getting under his fingernails. He had never hated and feared someone as much as he did Theodore right then.

He didn't know what to say, still afraid somehow that the bartender, who was now looking out the open door into Beadle Street, might hear them somehow despite the fact Marvin knew he hadn't been able to hear any of what the two of them had said a moment ago. So he merely nodded, and then looked down at this now empty glass of whiskey. He wanted a nap, and he wanted this man out of his life, and more than anything he wanted the event tonight to arrive.

"I take it you're not happy to see me."

"I should say not," Marvin said softly, knowing Theodore would hear him, only just barely. He was still looking into the empty glass. He wondered how hard he would have to hit Theodore in the head with the glass to kill him. Too hard, surely.

"I needed to get out and see the village," Theodore said, and Marvin could tell he was still staring at him. Sizing him up. Looking into him for something he could use or appraise. Marvin always felt like he was under a magnifying glass, naked, for Theodore, as though the man were examining everything Marvin had

Chapter 11

ever thought and said and did and considering it deliciously hilarious. He'd tolerated it for the first few weeks, especially after their engagements had begun to pay into the third digit, but in a moment like this it became to him quite possibly the most evil quality he'd ever experienced in another human being.

"And so that's what I did. Don't be ruffled, partner. Tonight will go over well enough. This fellow behind me is aiming to come himself."

Marvin's blood all dropped to his knees and his face suddenly looked the color of a corpse's. "You don't mean you told him I'm the one putting it on?"

"I did," Theodore said, and smiled the most loathsome smile Marvin had ever seen. He was still staring at Marvin, staring into Marvin, in a way that made Marvin's chest tighten and his scalp tingle. For the second time he wondered, almost aloud, *who is this man?*

"No need to worry," Theodore said, then looked at something on the wall behind Marvin. Marvin never turned around, so he had no idea what it was or if it mattered. When Theodore looked back into Marvin's eyes, his own glittered from behind his silver-framed glasses, and he smiled wider. "He'll never see *me*."

With that, Theodore stood up and walked the twenty feet to the bar, where he left a single bill on its surface and said something to the bartender. He walked out without looking back, and Marvin quickly decided it would be best to wait at least fifteen minutes before leaving himself.

He made no eye contact with the bartender.

12

1892

Josiah and Raymond shared a cup of coffee the next morning in the kitchen of Raymond's small house. Raymond was as tired as he'd ever been, having sat up most of the night with Rachel as the pain in her arm made it impossible for her to sleep. Her forehead had felt feverish, but when Josiah checked in on her in the morning, he became confident it was an effect of the broken bone in her arm, and that she was not otherwise ill. Raymond was relieved at that, greatly relieved considering the anxiety he now felt with any threat of illness, but he was still sleepless and felt vulnerable knowing that whatever had frightened Abigail Meyers the night before had also pushed his daughter to the ground so hard that it had snapped a bone in her. He had none of the reluctance to talk about it that he might have had otherwise. Demon or not, animal or not, he knew the thing must be destroyed, and he wanted to help Noel and any other men who would take up the charge.

"Do you have any further thoughts on what it is?" he asked Josiah plainly. He had taken a small drink of his coffee from the fine French ceramic mug in his hand that he had purchased in Baltimore three years earlier. Having swallowed it he felt somewhat normal for a moment. The warmth in his belly and the taste of coffee on his tongue was helpful.

"It isn't an animal," Josiah said, answering Raymond's first question.

"You're certain?" Raymond raised his thick black eyebrows, knowing Josiah was certain, but unable to stop himself from asking because of how much was at stake.

"Yes." Josiah looked back at him for a few seconds without saying anything, then continued. "It grabbed me around my lower leg. A firmer grip than a man's, but a grip. Thumbs, fingers, a hand. I felt them through my boot. They were thicker than the average man's, but it was a grip. It is not an animal."

"Then what?"

"If it is a man," said Josiah, taking a long drink of his own, "It's a bigger one than most. I think we have at least two pieces of evidence that would lead us to that conclusion. But if it's not a man, then I think we need to find it quicker. We have some idea of what to expect with a man. A man might be after money, he might be insane, he might enjoy frightening people. But we have some history, some ideas of what he might do, for how long, and what to prepare for. If it has the mind of a man, the intelligence of a man, but is something altogether different, we might have much more to lose. Much more at stake."

Chapter 12

Josiah's eyes didn't change much as he spoke, and Raymond was awed by that. His own heart felt as though it were on fire, and he had a tingling in his palms. There might be some sort of large, manlike creature digging up graves and carving up horses and it was stalking and terrorizing their town, and he had no idea what it was up to or what it was capable of. He felt a fear in himself that he couldn't remember ever having before. It felt as if he were choking on the reality of this thing. He took another drink of coffee just to have something to do, and then wondered what Josiah was feeling.

It would have surprised him to know that Josiah was scared.

* * *

At that moment the thing Josiah Hall and Raymond Stanton were scared of was eating. There was another cave a little less than two miles from the one Sidney Seagram and Joseph Carlysle had discovered in 1841. It was a larger cave, formed by the shelving of limestone walls on the southeastern side of a creek. It was forty feet deep, which was ponderously large for a natural cave in the region, and for the first thirty feet it was between six and seven feet high.

There was a fire burning in the back of the cave, two feet or so from where the jagged edges of dank limestone that reached into the hillside became too short for anything other than spiders and mice and cockroaches to continue. The shadows thrown up by the small flame were almost musically, rhythmically, dancing to the steady fire coming up from the burning wagon wheel that was unmoved by any air in the depths of the cave. There were drips of water, the small sound of the flame, and there was the wet smack of chewing. There were no other sounds. It seemed to be unbroken night back here. Rachel Stanton's hairpin glittered a little in the light of the flame, as did the eyes above it, and after two minutes the chewing stopped.

* * *

"You are willing to be responsible for him all night?" Noel had a look on his face that Bill Kline had never seen before, but he supposed that was to be expected.

"I am."

The sunlight was warm and good and healthy, spilling under the overhang in front of the door of Noel's office, and Bill felt it was strange for them to be housing a murderer and worrying about a grave robber or a vampire of some kind out there in those woods when everything was this bright and warm and he was only two months away from harvesting his corn. But Bill also believed his Bible, and believed what his pastor, Reverend Lowell, preached from it, and knew

Chapter 12

that God's earth was good and yet bad, that wicked things crept around on it. He just hated to see something so unpredictable come after his town, the town where his family lived, and to see it bring upon his friend this look he had now, and to force him to do whatever it was he would have to do. And, Bill believed, this thing had had some part in Ed Aimes being murdered by Hannibal, who was sitting back there in a locked room in the corner of Noel's office.

He watched his friend nod grimly, then turn out towards that sunlight. When Noel hesitated for a second before setting out down the two rickety steps that led to the road, Bill tried to think of something to say. He wanted Noel to think differently. He wanted Noel to be a Christian, truly Christian, but his mind felt thick as he looked at the back of his friend's head and knew that whatever happened later that day was going to be much too serious for Noel to want to hear anything Bill would have to say right now. And so Bill thought about Noel's sons, Stephen and Lawrence, and he prayed for them, and for their father, right there with his eyes open and the sun bright as gold and something terrible somewhere just outside of town for Noel to go get. Then he watched Noel step down into the street and head out southwest, through the town and towards what lay beyond it.

Noel felt the dirt under his boots as he walked out into the street, and he tried his best to ignore the

Nephilim

blister on his left heel. He took inventory of what he was confident was true. Something had run through town. It had wounded Rachel Stanton and had apparently intended harm to both Hannah Myers and Dr. Hall, whom it had begun to carry off into the woods. It was large, and it was a threat.

Not even his wife Patricia knew what God had woven into Noel's presence in what was happening in Sunbury. Noel's father knew that he had lied about his age in order to join the 27th Massachusetts in 1864, fourteen-years-old, but outside of his regiment no one else did. In June of 1864 he had held a rifle just outside of Petersburg, Virginia, and had put two bullets in the neck of a Confederate Corporal who had just turned to face him as he'd come over a hill covered in pale, green grass; grass that had been bending southeast in a breeze that carried the stench of powder mixed with the clean air from the open fields behind them. He'd fired the first bulled on reflex, before he'd had any time to think about it, at least in any way he could discern as thinking. But then the man, thick brown hair spilling out from underneath his cap and a beard that hadn't been shaved in what appeared to Noel to be months, a man's beard, a beard he'd have envied to see back at home, had pulled his side arm and was looking with eyes that had fire in them for who had fired into him. Noel had never seen eyes like that, rage and pain and fear of death, and so he pulled his own sidearm, dropping his rifle, and he

Chapter 12

pointed at the man's head but hit his neck again, not far from the first spot, and the man fell as though he had never been alive. He might as well have been a statue of a man. Noel looked down at him, but then he heard something fast and sounding like gunfire, and he got down as shots came over the hill from down below. Then he saw blue and gray blend above him, and something like a brick hit him in the head and he couldn't remember anything until he was with his friend Jonas Milbanks under a tent with heavy rain and the smell of smoke thick in his face. His first thought then, when he'd awoke, had been that the world was ending, and that he was in that eschaton himself. He was scared, because he knew what that would mean for him, and he'd reached for something next to him, having no idea what that would be. But there had been nothing there, and then he'd recognized Jonas' face above him. He'd felt Jonas' older boy's hands gripped around his right upper arm, and they were tight enough that he stopped moving. And then finally something about the rain pattering in the grass outside had made Noel realize there was no battle and no world ending, and that he was in a tent.

It had been a month after Appomattox that he had sat with Jonas in a tavern in Boston and asked him how he planned to go back to being a man out in the world again. He'd smiled, and picked up his glass of Scotch whiskey and tasted it, then put it back down.

Then he stopped smiling, and Noel had realized Jonas had killed a man, too, and that they could perhaps figure this out together.

"We were soldiers, Noel," he said, and then something seemed to change on his face, and he got up and walked across the tavern to a friend they'd known from Springfield. Jonas seemed to want to hear whatever story their friend was telling, but Noel knew. He knew what was really happening with his friend then, and he'd looked down at the table, wondering whether ignoring it might be the sounder judgment. But all he could think about was that he was alive and that Confederate Corporal was dead, and that that should be an unlikelier thing than it was.

Noel still believed in the War, and he was content with his having fought in it. What had never settled in his mind was what to do with every wicked thing in him that led up to those shots, and everything that had come after. Those two bullets seemed to be only the loudest reports in a life he knew had been wracked with things he was ashamed of, and other things he should be ashamed of but wasn't. Since the year or so after the war had ended, he had tried to be all that he could be by way of right behavior, not drinking and not fooling with women and being the sort of man he figured might be worth being, a man worthy of the family he'd made and the town where he'd settled. But all of his sins still scratched away at the back of his mind and he

Chapter 12

had no idea what he was to do with them. And without giving it much due thought, he had fallen into doing what Jonas had done that day in the tavern.

There was a grove of apple trees untended on the southeastern edge of Sunbury, and Noel made his way there now, without knowing exactly why. He knew what he would do tonight, he knew what he believed would happen with whatever was out in their woods. But he also felt certain that he owed it to himself, to something, to walk out there and be alone and consider what debts there might be to pay. It seemed to him he had to try to square away whatever was giving him this anxiety, whatever ghosts haunted him.

It was thick warmth out in that grove, the warmth of wool blankets or being right up close to a fireplace, and yet he sat out there without any discomfort under the shade of those apple trees. Like a good many men who say they doubt there is a God, Noel was in point of fact angry at God, and he was angry because he was afraid. There is a very real sense in which Noel Flagler actually knew the character of God more than some of the members of Reverend Lowell's church. But he wouldn't admit any fears of God or guilt, not now when the only man he knew how to be when there was anything at stake didn't confess fears or faith. He bore up, and he saw what had to be seen before others saw it. Well, before others excepting Dr. Hall.

Nephilim

There were two reasons he'd come here, to this spot where he sat now just southeast of the edge of town. The first was that he'd asked Patricia to marry him right here in the thick of this grove. It had been September, and the apples had been the color of blood, and they'd picked a basketful. He'd squared himself up, took a single bite of an apple that turned out to have a soft spot just under the skin, and he'd decided he couldn't rightly spit it out now that he'd begun to say the hardest thing he'd ever had to say. So he'd chewed it twice, and it had had the texture of a well-cooked sweet potato, and he must have made a face about it despite his best efforts, because Patricia suddenly started to laugh. Noel had felt he had two choices, and he should have known by this point that he'd made the wrong one, but he didn't know it. He hadn't laughed with Patricia, instead he'd gotten a bit red in the cheeks, and then he'd taken another bite, as though he were proving to himself or someone else that he had things under control, then he'd told her of his plans and that he'd talked to her father and that he'd like to have her hand in marriage. But he was frustrated by her laughing, and she was still smiling. Then she'd put her left hand on the apple tree he was leaning back against and she'd said, "Well, Noel, you still haven't asked me." He'd felt like he'd taken another bad bite out of that apple. He made a face that said as much, and they almost argued, though he was able to apologize without apologizing, a

Chapter 12

gift of his, or at least a skill he'd honed, and eventually she smiled and agreed she did want to marry him. But some of the goodness of the moment had bled out because of his pride and his fear, and he was here now because he loved her and was worried about her and the boys, and he had some crazy feeling he was going to die soon somehow with all of this. And that his pride and fear might leave something unpleasant behind.

The other reason was more tactical. Josiah Hall and Raymond Stanton had told him earlier that day about Sidney Seagram's old papers. Noel hadn't given it much consideration when he was with them, and he still wasn't sure that something fifty years ago had anything to do with graves being robbed and a bear or something like a bear hurting women at night now, but he was sure he had to go look at those places. And that he wouldn't tell either man about it. He hadn't told anyone, actually. Noel still harbored a stubborn hope that they were dealing with an animal, and that some fool had robbed the graves.

He had hunted in these woods as much as anyone in Sunbury, even Joe Mertz. He knew the spot on the creek where that flour mill sat, covered in vines and with one wall, the south wall, completely collapsed. And he knew the hillside that the old cholera hospital sat under. He'd never gone near it, no one did, even among the handful of men he knew who hunted game out in that part of the woods or who lived in cabins on the edge of Fairhaven. They knew what the place was, and no one wanted to risk it. But it hadn't been in use since ten or fifteen years before Noel had been born, and he doubted he would contract the disease now that fifty or more years had passed since the last patient had been treated there. He would make his way to the hospital this afternoon, heading the three miles south into the woods it would take, and then turn west and try to find the cave Sidney Seagram once had.

Noel's heel still hurt, but he gave it no mind as he stood up from under the apple tree his wife had once put her hand on when she'd known but not yet said, and he scratched the back of his neck, right where his yellow hair stopped, and set out into the woods.

He'd noticed the quiet out in the woods yesterday, and while mid-day in high summer might be some of that, it was unusual. And he gave it enough weight in his mind to keep listening the entire three miles.

The hill was a hundred feet high or more, large enough to see from Fairhaven, which sat back on the edge of the woods about four miles east of Sunbury. The ground of Sunbury was a bit lower, and the woods seemed to tower above her, like a rising wave of dark green stretching out into the horizon, but the folk in Fairhaven knew the hill and knew that the hospital had once been in use there. Noel stepped out of the woods and into what remained of the clearing in what was still

Chapter 12

mid-day. The sun was thick and gave him the impression nothing of what he feared might actually be there, nor could it ever be. He was wrong, of course, but it's easy to understand. It was a golden day, and there was an orange-and-black butterfly making short rounds among a handful of wildflowers in front of the tall wooden fence around the old hospital's property. The fence had tall grass, cattails and even some sunflowers setting up shop around it, and the day seemed to be one made for sitting under the shade of the general store's overhang and smoking and making slow, good conversation with Bill and the other men who held court there on summer weekdays. It was the kind of a day on which he might walk with Patricia and the boys in the early evening, when the fireflies began to embark out over the thick green grass that blanketed the edges of town all the way up to the shore of the woods. He watched the butterfly for a few seconds, then walked up to the fence, eight feet high, and put his hand on the old wood, just underneath a vine as thick as his forearm, and had all the goodness of the day drain away. He had never been as sure of something that hadn't happened yet. He knew he was about to find something awful, though he'd have had no chance of explaining how he knew it to anyone who'd have asked.

He walked forward, keeping his right hand on the form of the fence, even as it ran across masses of the vines. The woods were getting further behind him now. He was looking for the gate, and he knew, as the tall blades of grass began to convert to shrubs and weeds that were almost up to his chest, that knowing where the middle of this fence was, the center of the property, wouldn't be easy. He could climb the hill and look down into the old hospital, but the hill was thickly wooded, with undergrowth that fought you every step. He had only ever made it a few feet up that hill from the other side, and even that had usually left him with scratches on his arms and face. He'd never been this far into the clearing that held this old property, but he still held that this was his best chance.

And then he found it. The gate had an arch that he hadn't expected to see, but the vines hadn't found enough structure there to reach up that high and own it. There were two metal poles that went up a foot above the top of the fence, and they supported a wooden arch that sat above what had once been the hospital's front gate. Noel pushed from directly under the center of that arch and was disheartened that nothing gave. It felt much like pushing on the trunk of a hundred-year-old tree. He gave it a moment's thought, then pulled out his knife and began hacking at the vines, determining that even if he could merely get to the raw wood of the thing, he could find a chance of finding some way in.

A cloud of insects disturbed him as he sliced his way through the thick green, and he even saw a black

Chapter 12

snake wiggle its way off in the direction of the woods as he cut, but he did eventually see the dark brown wood of the gate, and that gave him enough success to spend another thirty minutes clearing away the vines on the central part. When he found the latch, he was able to kick it off all together, and then pry the high right side of the gate back enough to squeeze into the property.

Noel had been on two battlefields, but had never felt like he did now. He knew already that Josiah was right. There was a brand of prescience that he'd sensed when out in battle that he would never have been able to translate, but it was the sort of feeling that convinced you, beyond any doubt, that you had to crouch low immediately. And so you did. Noel looked over tall grass inside that was up to his neck, and he saw the old stone facility stretching at least a hundred feet east to west along the foot of the hill, two stories, laid out in front of him, and he knew it was everything he feared.

It was quarried stone, and there were no buildings of that kind in Sunbury, so it was striking to see. The place had been built out here for good reason, but the stones that made her, dug out of the earth, seemed ugly to him for some reason. He stopped in what would have once been the courtyard, the hillside towering above him as he'd never experienced before, never having stood on the north side of its peak as he was now, and he weighed what was best. The hospital's front doors were there, old wood, paint long sunned and weathered off, and he could certainly get through one of the six broken first floor windows if need be. But he also nursed a solid confidence that there was nothing in that building that would tell him about whatever had long ago taken bodies out of the hospital's graveyard, before Sidney Seagram and his cohorts had returned them.

It was then that Noel heard a click, a sound he'd never heard before, and he felt a different sort of fear than he'd ever felt. He knew enough of the woods and the way sound carried through them to know that it was at least a hundred yards away, but it was not the sound of wood snapping. It was more metallic, more mechanical, and every hair on his arm and on his neck had risen. But he had come here, and if he left now, if he surrendered to fear or even to an actual monster of some kind out there in the woods, he would have proven something he couldn't stand to be true, and he would have wasted what he'd spent. He knew the cemetery would be behind the facility. And so as quietly as he could, Noel walked along the front of the building until he came to the corner of its old stone face in about four minutes.

Before making his way around the side, he breathed in as much as he could of the air, fresh and warm and having all the qualities of the summer he judged worthy. It smelled like life, he thought. Then he began the trek through the tall grass that was in

Chapter 12

shadow, tucked between the old fence eight feet or so to his left and the side wall of the building. Here he was walking through a crowded mist of insects, and he heard several birds calling out to each other from within the building, their sounds echoing off the old stones in what struck him as an attempt of life's broaching what had been sickness and death, and now was just memory. When he made the last several steps into what was behind the building, taking up the last hundred yards of ground clutched up at the foot of the hillside, it only took him two or three seconds to know what he was seeing, and to know that it was everything he'd feared.

Holes in the earth, as though two dozen fingers had reached down from the heavens and pierced the soil as deeply as they could, were everywhere. Noel scanned the flat field that went all the way up to the tangled deep green of vines and shrubs that had overtaken the back section of fence that had once been the rear of the facility. He saw a few small wooden placards still standing, all in front of open graves. Throughout, there were uneven piles of dry dirt that held small strips of growing grass. As best he could judge, there wasn't a single grave that hadn't been unearthed. He had never used the word "unholy" before, but it was the word for what had been done here, what this place had become. There was something like what Dr. Hall feared, and it had inflicted itself on this place. A wolf would kill, a bear would kill, a cougar would kill. But it took something with anger, something with an intent to be wicked, something with a malignant design, in order for this to be waged. It was a flat note sung willfully against the world, not the call of a mere animal intelligence.

Noel walked on because he had already come all this way, but they were the hardest steps he recalled ever having taken. His legs felt liquid, and his hands and ears and eyes were sensitive to everything around him. He made his way around the edge of what had once been the cemetery, keeping more than a stone's throw to the left side, just inside the old fence. He could see even from here that the piles of dirt had settled, and that grass had begun to grow on them, but they still showed as distinct from the topsoil underneath them. He figured the graves couldn't have been dug up any more than five years ago. That meant that it had happened a second time, long after this place had been shuttered, and fifty years after Seagram and the others from Sunbury had put the bodies back the first time.

The other fact that he took account of was that the fence was intact all the way around, stretching the entire way back to the hillside and around the rear of the property. There was no rear gate that he could see, and the front gate he had just cut and fought his way through had been shut for at least a decade. Probably much longer. And so something had gotten in here

Chapter 12

without walking in the usual way, and had dug up these twenty or thirty graves, and had then gotten back out with the remains however it had gotten in.

Noel got to the back fence and stared up at the hillside. There were no paths up there, nothing but green packed so tight against other green that he doubted a fox could make the journey to the top. He walked west, keeping his hand against the back fence, searching for any place where it had been broken or had collapsed. He kept his eyes to his right, though, watching ceaselessly in the direction of the building for any sign of movement. About halfway along the fence, where there was a small shrub with branches thick enough that he figured it must be ten years old, he saw what he thought was a depression in the earth near the southwestern corner of the property, the back right if considered from the front of the hospital. He stopped watching the grounds to his right and looked intently at what he now thought was a sinkhole, at least ten feet in diameter. His heart began to beat much faster. Though he wouldn't admit it until he reached the edge, just inside both the south and eastern sides of the fence, he'd known from twenty paces away.

There was a single pile of earth against the rear section of fence, but it had been overgrown by grass now. It sat as a small, hip-high hill to his left, preventing him from touching the fence once he was within a few feet of the hole.

Nephilim

It was a tunnel.

* * *

His name was Randall Bostick. He had worked in Joseph Carlysle's mill right up to its closure in 1880. He was fifty-five now, and he'd hardened himself against his conscience enough to have lost no sleep about his having left his wife Maggie and their three daughters and one son behind in Rhode Island and come back to the Berkshires for no other reason than restlessness. He had told his wife that he had a summer and autumn job in logging out this way, and that he'd be back before Christmas, but he had no intention of ever going back. He did know a man in Sunbury whom he was planning on locating before autumn, but his first stop was going to be the mill. He knew it hadn't been in use for twelve years, and he was intimately aware of every spot in the building. He could live there for a few weeks, maybe more, and be very comfortable. The creek was no doubt still running, even in high summer it was at least two or three feet deep of good clean running water, and he could hunt game with the long rifle he'd brought.

Randall had entered the woods just south of Fairhaven, and it had taken most of the morning, tired as he was, to get to the creek. He remembered the bend where he had picked it up, and he knew that he had a mile further south to tread before reaching the mill. The

Chapter 12

trees thinned out a bit as he neared the bank of the creek, but he was still in plenty of shade, and so he decided to take his boots off and sit on its bank and let the water run over his feet as he put his back on some soft soil and rested for a spell. He found a spot that pleased him after three or four minutes of looking and unlaced his boots and placed them in front of the thin tree to his left and put his feet in the water, moving quickly enough that he felt better in only a few seconds. He lay back on the thin grass and soft forest floor and closed his eyes.

He fell asleep almost immediately, though he hadn't intended to. So when his mind first registered a thick crack, it simply became an unsettled part of a dream he was having. But by the second crack, coming as it was from much closer, he was awake. He immediately grabbed his rifle. Randall had been a hand in a railyard for a year in Colorado when he was twenty-seven, and he had killed a man for trying to steal his wallet and his sack one night near Boulder. He had run, and that was the end of it as far as the law was concerned, but that night was what was on his mind when he grabbed the rifle and held it out away from him in the direction of the sound. He was ready to fire. But he wasn't sure what he was looking for.

The shadows were thick, even though it was early afternoon, a hundred yards or so behind him and away from the stream, and that was where the sound had come from. He held the gun steady and pointed it in that direction. He shouted. He didn't hear anything for a few seconds. Then there came a quick succession of sounds to his left, in the opposite direction. Cracking sounds, the sounds of sticks breaking and larger wood snapping. Then he was sure he heard it above him, and he thought for a moment that he might be hearing an animal, and the thought actually relieved him enough that he smiled. It was a sick looking smile, because his face had become craven enough and greedy enough through the last thirty years of looking hungrily for what he could stash away for himself that even smiling under his black beard seemed to be a gesture of violence. But then he knew it wasn't an animal, because he heard it slow down as it got closer to him, and then it was in the treetops just above him, the elm trees with tops forty feet above his head. He didn't look up, as much from confusion as from fear. Then there was a splash in the creek, a splash like the sound of a wagon or a horse being dropped into the water from way up there, and he looked immediately, and he'd never seen anything like it. He tried to scream, but it was too late.

* * *

Noel ran his right hand along the edge of the tunnel. He was crouching, and his light jacket was scraping the lowest parts of the tall blades of grass that grew right up

Chapter 12

to the edge. With the sun behind him and shining down into it, he could see that it was dug clean and precisely, like a mine shaft; better, even. And it went down a solid six feet or more before pushing west, out under the fence and back into the woods. As terrified as he was, he did actually consider dropping down into it, but there was no telling where it actually led, how it actually terminated, and he'd have no way out again if he needed to come back up the same way he went in. It was a sheer vertical drop down walls of dirt and stiff clay.

He looked down into the shadows at the bottom, curious as to whether there was standing water down there from rainfalls, but he didn't see sunlight reflecting off any liquid. He was amazed at what he was seeing, but he was also aware of what it meant. He looked up at the treetops towards the peak of the hill, and he felt the copper and heat and confusion of that guilt he was always running from, and being as stubborn as he was, he gave it no thought and instead decided to kick his way through the tall grass and into the hospital itself. He had at least seven hours before he had to be where he intended to be that evening, and it was only a thirty-minute walk to the mill from here.

He made his way through the dense green on the western edge of the cemetery, looking three times to his right at the emptied graves from this side for the first time. He counted seven wooden grave markers that remained upright, but none had any writings or carvings he could discern from this far away. By the time he was within ten feet of the covered area that must have at one time served as the hospital's rear porch, he was looking only at the building. There were eight stone columns that held up a thin roof that extended five feet or so out from the rear wall of the hospital. He could see from here there was no true floor to the covered area, though he suspected that at one point there may have been stone tiles or wooden planks to walk on. He could see from a distance that the tiles on the porch's roof remained, and that would have surprised him if he hadn't already known the fear that this place evoked in the folks who knew it was out here. No one wanted the sort of sickness that had once been quartered here.

He stepped under the overhang and looked down at the crabgrass and vines that were finding a home in the perpetual shade on the back porch. He didn't see anything he would consider evidence of this beast's presence this close to the building, but he suspected he would inside. He had a kind of fear he could do nothing with but ignore, a fear that was a blood cousin of the one he always felt, and that he always ignored. There was a demon or a ghoul haunting the bones of this old place, and for all he knew it was waiting for him inside. He counted the broken windows, decided to try the large back doors before going through any of those

Chapter 12

three, and found that the old brass handle still functioned as it would have fifty or more years ago.

The door pulled out without any extra effort, and he stepped inside the building quickly, so as not to give himself any chance to consider the alternative. It felt odd to be back in the shadows again, and the smell was strange. He could tell there had been medicines, and alcohol, but the main scents seemed to be rot and animal urine. Once his eyes adjusted to the shadows there was just enough sunlight that made it in the front windows, totally exposed to the sun and with no porch to shade them on that side of the building, that he could see the entire first floor was essentially open. There were four doors that must lead to inner rooms, two on either side, but they were each forty feet or so from where he stood in the center of the building. He guessed that they led to small rooms on the two outer edges of the hospital, and that where he stood now was a sort of open living and eating area. There were five long tables, each probably fifteen feet end-to-end, and a stone fireplace on the eastern wall to his right. But there were almost no chairs or any other furniture remaining.

He walked as silently as he could, regularly looking to the left and right at the four doors, as well as to the stone staircase to his left in the northwestern corner. He wanted to get to the front entrance and read what was carved into a single circular stone piece above the high doors.

He stood just inside the ten-foot-high wooden front doors and read it with a sort of reverence he had never sensed in himself before.

"For he must reign, till he hath put all enemies under his feet. The last enemy that shall be destroyed is death." First Corinthians 15:25-26

What manner of place was this?

Despite Noel's general obtuseness about such things, he would have been ready to admit the sacredness of the place if asked. If for no other reason than for the contrast it bore to the foul sight of human graves violated as they had been outside. But that wouldn't have been the only reason. He was looking at the wooden cross that was hung just above the passage from the New Testament, and he had such a sense of being a guest on someone else's ground that, had he been a boy, he would have run and hidden. He would never have said that last part aloud, but he felt down in the tips of his fingers that it was true.

He looked away from the cross and towards the two doors on the west side of the building and the steps that led to the second floor. One of the doors was open a few inches, and he walked slowly and quietly over to it, glad with each step that the floor was stone and not wood. He doubted at this point that the creature was in here now, but every hair on his neck and arms was still standing, and his heart was beating as though he'd just run a footrace. When he reached the door he looked

Chapter 12

through the two inches or so of that it was ajar. There was a table that had nothing on it but two simple white cups, one on either side, as though two friends had been sharing tea before they vanished, along with most of the hospital's furnishings and supplies. He stepped over to the left door, tried its bronze knob, and found it locked. He guessed that whatever was inside was not worth the risk and the work that breaking into the room would involve, and so he turned to the staircase.

He was able to walk up the steps without making any noise, but when he reached the point where he could look up over the top step and see into the second floor, he was exceedingly slow. He couldn't dispel the image of the thing, whatever it was, hulking and black and giant and with the ivory, finger's-length fangs of a lion, perched a few feet from the top of the staircase, waiting patiently for him. But when he reached the top, he simply saw a long hallway stretching out away from him across the entire second story, and individual doors lining either side. Every single one was opened. He guessed that there were about twenty small apartments, and with slow and quiet steps he walked the entire length of the hall and looked in each.

Most retained the metal bed frame that each patient would have slept on, and three or four of them still had a small piece of furniture or two, a table or a plain wooden chair or a small bookcase. He had a sadness that surprised him as he looked into each successive room, imagining a patient in each one looking out his or her window and out into the green of the woods stretching out towards Fairhaven or, for the rooms on the right side of the hall, over the cemetery and then at the hillside. He expected at least several of those here at any given time would have died here, without kin or friends or neighbors, and that tapestry in his mind as he took each step affected him to such an extent that he forgot to be afraid. Once he was sure the rooms had nothing to tell him, he sat down on the top step of the staircase and simply breathed and gave himself time to consider what was next.

He was confident the creature had not been inside the building, now. And he had trouble accounting for the fact. He doubted it opened and shut doors, seeing that, as fantastic as the thought seemed, it had crafted a tunnel as its entrance into and exit from the facility. And both doors into the hospital building itself had been shut. The windows were likely large enough for a man to get in through, but if Dr. Hall were right about the marks on the tree they'd seen being from whatever had done this, it was much larger than a man. And even then, almost every one of the broken windows still had sizable shards of remaining glass in its frame. Noel was left with the conclusion that the creature had stolen bodies from the hospital's cemetery twice, but had never come into the hospital itself. He picked up a single white cloth, a bit thicker

Chapter 12

than a handkerchief. It had been sitting on the step where his feet rested. He opened it as he thought, just wanting to feel something in his hands as he gave consideration to an idea that hadn't taken on words yet. He opened the cloth, saw no stains of any kind, folded it neatly, and set it on his right leg.

He looked at it for less than a minute, and then he knew.

"It's afraid to come in here," he said out loud.

He was confused by this, but he was certain.

It was afraid of the same thing he was.

* * *

Noel found Sidney Seagram's cave within a few hours of leaving the old hospital grounds. He had guessed the bodies weren't there by the time he was up to the crack Seagram had described, and once he was inside, he confirmed it. There was nothing down in it but some puddles of rank water. But his fortune in finding it more quickly than he'd expected gave him the pluck to search out the bluffs in the area for another cave the beast might have used. And that was how he discovered its den.

The entrance was a simple cave, but the slanted tunnel it had carved down into the earth and clay from there was its own work. And he was certain it would have taken it years. Noel had brought his pistol, and he

Nephilim

held it out every step down what seemed to him to be much too steep for ordinary steps. By the time he judged that he was thirty feet underground, he began to see the dancing light of a fire reaching up into the tunnel from somewhere below. He stopped where he was at that point for at least ten minutes, listening and watching for any sign of it, his pistol pointed down into the tunnel beneath him. After that, he continued his descent, and several minutes later he was in a large cavern, large enough that the fire burning at its center did not light up all its rounded stone walls.

He found no remains. But the three objects he did find, all placed a few feet from the wood fire in the center of the space, on a flat stone slab, he carried out as quickly and as quietly as he could. One was a hairpin. The other two had once belonged to Theodore McCabe.

* * *

"What do you make of this?"

Raymond Stanton was asking about the letter, if that is what it was. It was one of the three objects Noel had taken from the cave. The truth was that Noel didn't know what to make of it. He neither knew who Theodore McCabe was nor whether the thing was to be believed as factual history or taken to be the product of a drunken man or a would-be Edgar Allan Poe.

Chapter 12

"I think Dr. Hall would know better than I do."

They were sitting in Dr. Hall's office, with the remains of the afternoon's sun casting a healthy glow into what struck Noel as an otherwise gloomy room. He'd acknowledge, though, that seeing Ed Aimes die here the day before may have given him an unfair judgment on the place.

Raymond looked over at Josiah Hall, sitting next to him and opposite Noel. He suspected Noel was right, even if he weren't quite sure why.

"It sounds to me like what we are looking at is essentially the last testament of a troubled criminal soul who somehow crossed paths with our monster." He paused, but without shifting or giving any visible sign of his thinking. That habit of his, of always considering and thinking deeply but never looking as though he were, had always made Noel nervous.

"It seems," Dr. Hall continued, "that he found the creature much the same way you did, Noel. Or at least in the same manner as that in which you found its home."

"I don't rightly know what I found," Noel lied, mostly to himself.

"I suspect you do," Dr. Hall answered, and then looked over at Raymond. "I think we know by now that we are bound to kill this creature. We have no other option but to find it and destroy it, knowing what we do now about its intents and its capabilities."

Nephilim

Neither Raymond nor Noel disagreed with this, but the feeling of what Noel had seen being real was more than either man was able to translate into action at the moment. They both sat in the simple wooden chairs in Dr. Hall's packed office, vials and medical volumes and papers lining most of the spaces along the walls and covering all of his tables and his desk, looking at each other and trying to decide whether they could really believe any of this. Raymond was able to decide more quickly.

"Let's get our rifles," he said, and stood up and walked to Dr. Hall's front door.

"I have a plan for tonight," Noel offered both men, "and it's one I already have assistance for. But you men are welcome to do as you see fit, especially in defending your homes." Raymond looked as though he were going to object, but held his peace, likely deciding that Noel was no coward and must mean, more or less, what he said. He nodded and opened the door of Dr. Hall's office and held it, waiting for Josiah to rise from his own chair.

"Noel?" Dr. Hall asked from behind him.

"Yes?" He turned and faced Josiah Hall.

"Thank you," Dr. Hall said, and extended his right hand to him.

Noel was struck by the warmth such a pensive man could convey in a few words and a simple bodily gesture. He was as affected by that action from Josiah

Chapter 12

Hall as any he could remember. He took the doctor's hand in his own, and the two nodded at each other as they shook.

Noel made for the door first, seeing as Raymond was holding it open. As he passed Raymond and put his right foot out into the sunlight, he pulled the other object he'd found in the cavern out of his right pocket and looked down at it, somberly. Then he handed it to Raymond.

"This was down there, too," he said. "Maybe the fellow who wrote that was able to do with it what he set out to."

Raymond looked at it with wonder, and then put his right hand on Noel's left shoulder and nodded his head.

Noel returned the nod, and then stepped out into the open air of Beadle Street, hoping to do what he needed to quickly in order to be ready for tonight.

13

1843

Marvin's act that second night at the Sunbury Inn was stunning. A young widow was there, her face pale as ivory from fear of what she was attending and exhaustion from finding her first week of being a widow populated by the death of a neighbor and her town vibrating with anxiety as it braced, it seemed, for more to come. Her eyes were bloodshot and she wore a plain black blouse and she wouldn't make eye contact, even when Marvin responded to her payment with his most sympathetic, "My dear, I truly hope that we obtain some comfort for you." She made him nervous for a few seconds, but when she broke down into quiet sobs a moment later in her chair at the big table facing a wall, so as to hide it from the other guests, he felt better. She was no spy or "exposer;" she felt guilty. He knew the look of a person who was ashamed to be associating with the darker arts. She was no threat to his operation. She would eventually settle in, get what she paid for, and leave quietly and with gratitude. She wasn't a threat to his act.

The evening was filled with more raw anticipation than he had ever experienced. It felt like the air just before a brutal thunderstorm. Eleven of those present were there, having paid willingly, merely to hear if any of the recently departed might tell them what danger or

Chapter 13

pestilence might be stalking the town. Was an outbreak of the fever to coil itself around them, taking the young and old first and then striking the rest as they grieved? Was this a divine judgment they might avert? Another nine, including the widow Marvin had first noticed, were there to hear from their loved ones who had died. The Bloomfields wore the typical expressions of hosts who had adopted Marvin and his routine: Excited smiles and knowing glances at the new guests, as though they themselves had spoken to the dead and had information to share. Marvin indulged them with a gracious, discreet nod at the beginning of the event and once more when Theodore was rattling the window in the room from the outside. They would have made Marvin their sole heir at that point had he asked. They were mesmerized by him and felt as important as they ever had to be a part of his supernatural doings.

Marvin was at the last of his tricks, the discerning of a message to Mrs. Joy Appleby from her deceased husband John about their son who had moved to Chicago, information Theodore had covertly gathered along with the other required details about several guests present, when the sounds on the roof started.

It began as a series of heavy thuds above them, five or six in all, each with a second or two between it and the next. Marvin stopped talking after the third, and everyone was looking up at the ceiling by then. A thin mist of dust was falling towards them all, just visible in the light of the three oil lamps in the Bloomfields' front room. The last of the dust had just dispersed onto the surface of the table when they all heard what sounded to Marvin to be the loudest cow he had ever heard.

It was a long, stable note that rose quickly to a pitch where it then rested and held for what he was sure had to be fifteen seconds. It made his heart seem to stop, and he had to resolve to himself that he was not in a nightmare. Several of the people jumped, and he heard two of the women scream, but Marvin's outward comportment was simply stable. He kept his left eyebrow raised as he composed himself in order to maintain what he knew was required of him. To everyone but him (and Theodore outside), this was a feature of the supernatural occurrences Marvin's gift had brought about, occurrences they had sought him for and asked he bring about, and he would protect that illusion until everything short of his physical life was threatened.

After a moment of silence, Marvin opened his eyes slowly and, he hoped, with an appearance of wisdom and intention. Then, as discreetly as he could, he looked over to the window where he hoped Theodore might still be positioned. But there was only the black night beyond the glass, and even that was obscured by the reflection of one of the lamps. He moved his eyes down to the book he was holding, as

Chapter 13

though the answer to what they'd all heard lay in there, and he opened to the page he usually did when something slightly unexpected happened.

"There is something I did not anticipate that is happening tonight, friends," he said, with the same weight and seriousness he always did. "The involvement of our loved ones from the other side, and the forces none of us yet adequately understand, have begun to rupture what we are experiencing. We m-"

The thud came from the roof directly above them, now, and was violent enough to shake the table and cause three more women to scream. Marvin controlled his body the way he always did, but his eyes did look up, while his neck and head stayed exactly where they were. He had no idea what was happening.

From where he stood at the head of the table, Marvin breathed deep and closed his eyes and started to speak to the dead again. *Always use the rifle you trust,* he told himself. He began to ask the dead to give them only the truest assurance that they were safe and aware of their friends' and families' affections for them from this side of the grave. An old woman with a missing front canine and deep gray hair, gray so deep it seemed to have an almost blue hint to it in the light of the lamps, began to cry. Her eyes looked back and forth between a handful of people at the table she evidently knew. "What is it? What is happening up there?"

Nephilim

"Friends," Marvin began, but that was when the window in the kitchen broke open, and the old woman shrieked in such a squealing manner that Marvin winced. It was his first show of anything other than calm and wise composure. Things were getting quite out of hand, and if he could, he would call the whole event off at this point. But there was no way to do that and still ensure future meetings, which he could not give up. He had never had an opportunity like this one, before, an entire town wound up to a pitch of unparalleled anxiety who all wanted to talk to the dead. But then the sound came again, and this time it was just outside the broken window, and it wasn't only women screaming now.

14

1892

Rachel didn't wake up from the sound, though for a moment she thought she had, or that the sound itself was the tail of a nightmare that was just slipping out of the light of her memory forever. She had actually awakened two or three seconds before it.

Her face was tight, and her eyebrows furrowed from the pain in her left arm. She still felt feverish, weak and with her forehead damp and the tips of her fingers and toes feeling chilly. The sound reminded her of a horn, but not a brass one that a man in an orchestra or a band might play. It sounded like a wooden horn she had once seen at the home of her father's friend Mr. Bishop, long ago when she was a girl. It had been made from old, dark wood, and Mr. Bishop, who was a gentle and kind soul but who had always smelled of tea and so made younger Rachel a combination of nervous and nauseated, had explained to her that it was from the Algonquian tribe of Indians. He had let her blow into it, and she had lit up when she heard the sound it made from just a bit of air from her tiny, little girl lungs and lips. It was rough and ancient to the touch, so to hear such a powerful and musical sound from it, a sound she had made herself using it, had been delightful. She'd laughed and played with it for several minutes before her father made her give it back. She had enjoyed every second. It had made a lasting impression on her, and it came back into her memory now before the sound far away outside faded.

It wasn't the same sound as last night she decided. It was too steady. It must have been a horn of some kind, and a horn would belong to a person, a normal and safe person who simply had occasion to use a horn, or a similar instrument. The fact that it was night notwithstanding, she informed herself over and over again that that was what she heard.

Having settled that as best she could in her mind, however, she found she was still frightened. It was in large part because the room was dark, and she was in pain, and, upon waking up, the agony in her arm and the stiff darkness had left her with the impression that, somehow, she was back in the events of the night before, outside in their grass and hoping that the Cartwrights would notice her and that whatever had injured her would not come back. It took thought, now, thought she hadn't had to spare until the sound had been gone for a minute or two, to remember that her father had been away with Dr. Hall and Noel Flagler all day. Once she did remember and form a good shape of where and when she was in her mind, she also thought about Mrs. Tufts, who would be here somewhere, probably sleeping in her father's room or out in the front room of the house reading or sewing. Her father had asked Abigail Tufts to stay with Rachel, and Mrs.

Chapter 14

Tufts had been happy to do so. She was here in the house. That made Rachel feel much better, and she decided to get out of the bed.

The pain in her arm as she stood up was a kind of fire, a fire on the inside of her skin spread up to the top of her neck. She screamed just a bit, but she cut it short with a grunt and clenched her stomach tightly when she heard the sound on the roof.

It was a hard thud, as though someone had just dropped a load of lumber or a wheelbarrow filled with stones onto the top of their house, and it was just above her bed. For a moment, Rachel thought it was a sort of earthquake, or that the house was falling down, but there was silence for several seconds after that and she collected her thoughts and ordered them. *Something is on the roof. Something heavy just dropped onto the roof right over my head.*

She heard smaller thuds and creaking, moving across the roof in the direction of the front of the house, which was to her back now the way she had gotten out of bed. Then, after a few seconds, the thuds stopped, and she prayed.

Almighty God, hear me, please. Whatever is on our roof, if there is anything there, do not let it kill me or Mrs. Tufts or father or anyone else. Please protect us, our Lord.

Rachel had sudden onsets of feelings and thoughts and convictions while she was praying. This had happened for as long as she could remember, perhaps as far back as when she was three or four years old. She would deliver words, like little parcels wrapped and held dearly against one's chest, to her Father in Heaven, as Raymond had taught her to pray, and in the quiet moments after the last word she would rest under the warmth of something from Him. Often it was too immense, too profoundly real and good, to describe other than by analogy. Had she spoken about those experiences, she might have said something like, "It feels like being outside on a clear morning at the beginning of a holiday, and the sun is just right there coming up over the eastern edge of ground, and there is a bird that is singing and just the slightest chill in the air and everything is right and ahead of you." Or she might have spoken what it seemed to be in Paul's Epistle to the church in Rome: "For ye have not received the spirit of bondage again to fear; but ye have received the Spirit of adoption, whereby we cry, Abba, Father." Or that it had the smell and sense of her father's embraces, the ones that were tight and wordless and always contained a bit of himself in them, left behind as he stroked the back of her head and then kissed her cheek.

She felt something like that now, standing under the sounds that had shaken her in the darkness of her bedroom, but it was firmer and sterner and had a different sort of weight to it. She felt just as sure that her Maker and Savior was with her in every real manner

Chapter 14

she needed, but it was a different sort of preparation for her soul than she had felt in the past. Where she often felt gratitude for the goodness at hand, joy at the simplicity of her prayer answered with tenderness from a very real God, she now felt as though it was time for something hard to begin, and that she would not have any certainty as to what to do until the moment came, but that it would matter very much, and that the things beginning to happen to her would scare her.

I don't know what it is. But if I am supposed to do something, Lord, I will.

She stood quietly, hoping not to make any sounds, then turned her body towards the window in her bedroom, and she saw on the other side of the glass its round eyes, eyes with no irises and thick black pupils that seemed unimaginably large. Then she heard what to her seemed like thunder, and the eyes were gone, and she heard a man's shout in the distance.

* * *

It was like looking at an oil slick on dark, tumultuous water. The thing was gone at least half a minute before Noel reached the spot where it had been standing. And he smelled what he thought must be it. It was pungent, but not altogether unpleasant. He grimaced as he tried to place the smell and stared out over the night in the

Nephilim

direction of the south edge of town. *Wet coffee grounds,* he thought. *It's the aroma of wet coffee grounds or tea leaves.*

Noel wiped his mouth with his right hand, knowing he'd finally seen whatever it was, placed it right here near where it had entered the town from the woods the night before, and satisfied with himself that he'd been right about where it would come. He'd been on Miles Cartwright's porch since a few minutes after sundown, slowly sipping the cup of coffee Joan Cartwright had brought him earlier. He hadn't told Rachel Stanton, or Raymond, for that matter, because he wanted her to go about her normal business, so to speak. That had been an instinct, too, though he hadn't had the courage to dwell on it. A bear roaming around for its next meal might enter the town at the same spot twice, maybe many times. But a bear wouldn't be stalking an individual townsperson. Noel thought about his two sons again, the image of their hair, the same shade as their mother's, holding him still for a second. Then he put his mind on what he had to do next, calling out to Joe Mertz, who had been stationed a few houses away at his cousin Frank's house. The window had been left open so he could hear Noel call should he see the thing, and so less than a minute later Joe was standing beside him with his dog. Noel smelled sweat and whiskey and looked over at Joe to make sure he was up for it, and he could tell he was, though what

Chapter 14

Noel really needed was the dog. But Joe was a sturdy enough fellow, and regardless it was too late now.

"See it?" asked Joe, looking steadily at Noel.

"Yes. I don't think anyone inside did, though. It was on the roof, then jumped down. I fired at it just after it was on the ground."

"On the roof?" Joe asked.

Noel nodded.

"What was that other noise? Long and loud? We heard it in the house. First, I thought I was hearing things, but then I figured as I was running over here it might have been you."

"It wasn't me," said Noel, and he started walking south, in the direction that the black thing had run, waving with his left hand for Joe to follow him. "That was it."

15

1843

Everyone in the front room of the Sunbury Inn was looking at Marvin. He had no ready answers, no counterfeit practiced explanations for what had occurred and, he was truly convinced, had nothing to do with Theodore. He was as scared as most of them, but he had kept his composure quite well, as most trained stage actors can do. Marvin was, after all, essentially a stage actor, though with the caveat that his audience never knew the play was fictional, or that it was intended to prey upon them. By now he had loosened his tie and removed his gloves, as though whatever had happened would require a bit more dexterity or informality to resolve. He didn't actually consider that with those small gestures he was trying to communicate that he had a plan, that there were steps to take, and he was prepared to take them, but that is what it was. A part of him just below the surface was aware that even if this house truly was haunted or there was a goblin assaulting the Sunbury Inn, he had to *appear* prepared to deal with such assaults. And if it were a burglar or a drunk or some less supernatural phenomenon, his early efforts in contacting the dead would still be respected, and they could all settle down to a nice laugh about how the end of the proceedings was a bit premature, and they should all revisit the next

Chapter 15

evening to take up where they left off. He had a nice set of disarming stories he could fall back to in having to adjourn early.

"What was it?" shrieked a yellow-haired woman in her forties who had been trying to reach her dead sister. "What was up on the roof?" Marvin had the sudden urge to murder the woman, but nothing more than a simple reassuringly raised hand happened for the group to see.

"I shall discover that presently, if you'll excuse me. Do not be alarmed, friends. There are many elements to my profession that we are only beginning to understand, but one thing is certain: With precision and great care I can restore our contact and keep us in the utmost safety. Allow me to step outside for a moment."

Everyone except for the young widow looked at him with admiration, despite the worry or even panic showing around some of their eyes, and he decided that regardless of what had really happened out there he had to collect his thoughts and find out for certain where Theodore was. He had his pistol in the small hip holster on his right side, and taking stock of it as he calmly made his way to the front door, he felt a bit better already.

Marvin shut the door behind him and stood out in the shadows, not moving, listening. The Inn was on Carpenter Street, a dirt path that was very wide for a street in Sunbury in those days. It stretched north into the heart of the town, which was about a fourth of a mile to Marvin's left. The street was perhaps ten paces in front of him, and the houses across it did not shed much light over here. The lamps in the windows across the way were points of light glimmering in the night; he could not see by them any more than by the stars overhead. The lamp in the window of the Inn behind him cast enough light to his left that as he turned his head slowly, he could see the individual blades of the tall, faded summer grass beneath the window. But beyond a few feet all was dark again. He listened, his head still pointing left, towards town. There were crickets, and far off in the distance he heard what sounded like the wheels of a wagon, but nothing else. No breeze, no sound of people out and about, and no sound of a man or a creature near the house. Cautiously, Marvin moved his right foot in front of his left, then the left in front of the right, and in a minute had made his way past the front of the house, where he looked down its length and squinted his eyes and focused, hoping and yet not hoping to see whatever it was that had caused the noises from the roof and broken the window.

There was nothing visible for a few seconds, but then he saw a flash of fire the size of a finger, and he gasped and jumped a few inches back. Instinctively, he reached for the pistol, but stopped when he heard, "It's

Chapter 15

me, Marvin. It's Theodore." Marvin felt only a small bit better, something which spoke to his heart in a way he resolved to reflect on later that evening. He quietly walked up to Theodore, stepping far enough away from the window in the broad side of the house as he did so that no one inside would have seen him approaching a co-worker for an apparently ordinary trade conversation. Theodore had no expression on his face above or below his beige mustache, at least none that Marvin could discern in the meager orange glow of the match he was holding under his chin. There was no breeze at all, and so the flame barely moved left or right. It was a steady vertical line in the reflection of Theodore's glasses that made it impossible to read his eyes. Marvin's chest was tight, tighter than it had been when he first stepped out the Inn's front door, but he had a wide blind spot when it came to Theodore, and he gave his anxiety no thought as he stepped up quietly towards him.

"That wasn't you, was it?" he asked, sounding more irritable and slightly less afraid than was reality.

Theodore shook his head, and now Marvin saw that there was actually a very faint smile on his lips, the right corner of his mouth drawn back and upward just enough to be noticeable in the light of the match.

"What was it?" Marvin asked, and looked up towards the roof, terrified to do so, and yet feeling he must.

Nephilim

His principal motive in anything and everything he did in Sunbury, or virtually anywhere else for that matter, was money. He could still have another event or two regardless of what happened out here. He had no reason to take up goblin hunting in the middle of the night, and he was thoroughly prepared to make another couple of nights' worth of revenue and leave town forever, probably with as much money as he'd made in the last year considering the fees he could charge tomorrow and the fact that the town was in such a state that he might be able to have forty guests. But here he was, looking up into the night, discerning nothing up there in impossible dark, only barely able to make out the outline of the roof of the Inn from the light of the two windows and Theodore's match. All of a sudden, he had the thought that he was dreaming, that there was no way any of this could really be happening, and then he felt a blinding sharp pain between his shoulder blades, and a hand over his mouth, and his back began to feel wet and warm. He tried to shout and threw up his right arm in a sort of a jab, but then everything was gone.

16

1892

Josiah and Raymond were in the building of the Presbyterian Church. It was night. They sat in a circle of light formed by Reverend Lowell's lamp sitting on the flat part of the pulpit above them, just a few inches above where his Bible and the text of his sermon would lay that coming Sunday. Francis Lowell was seated in a chair closest to the pulpit, while Raymond and Josiah faced him a few feet away. Raymond was tired and appeared anxious, which Reverend Lowell took (with good reason) to be concern for his daughter, whom he'd known had been injured the night before. Josiah looked much like he always did, serious and thoughtful and as though he had a question he wouldn't ask until he was good and ready. His red hair and mustache stood out against his plain brown jacket and dark brown hat (a hat he had not thought to remove) and his green eyes did the same. He was a striking man, Reverend Lowell noticed. "Striking" was a fitting word for Dr. Josiah Hall. Everything about him, except for his clothes he supposed, struck you, or at least did so if you took the time to watch him. Josiah made many men uncomfortable, because he seldom made small talk or joked or smiled, and that often gave men the impression that the doctor was appraising them, sizing up their moral stature and finding them wanting. He wasn't, he was merely almost always considering every angle of what was in front of him and what might be in front of him in the future, and he was also almost always praying silently. But he never said as much to anyone, not even his pastor, and so all Reverend Lowell knew was that Dr. Hall was humbler than he appeared to be.

"Do you remember anything about Sidney Seagram?"

Reverend Lowell nodded. "He was an ambitious man. He founded the bank and seemed to be an involved and wealthy man of business. He was a town trustee for a number of years. He had a wife and one son. A very serious man, but not unpleasant to talk to. I never had conversations of great spiritual depth with him, but he appeared to know who his Creator was and was a regular churchgoer here until his death something like twenty years ago." Reverend Lowell stopped, squeezed his hands together for a moment, and smiled grimly at Josiah. He knew there was something different the doctor was looking for, but he couldn't figure quite what it was just yet.

"Do you know about what he found out in the woods by the old Joseph Carlysle mill?"

"No," Reverend Lowell said, and squinted in confusion. "What was it?"

"Fourteen bodies in a cave. They'd been stolen from the graveyard of a Cholera hospital not far away

Chapter 16

and placed there. He kept at least some of it a secret, and from what he wrote down himself that I got from his son, he seems to have regretted that part."

Reverend Lowell stared thoughtfully at Josiah for several seconds, then asked when this had happened.

"1841," Josiah answered simply.

Raymond studied both men from his own place in the triangle of wooden chairs placed below Reverend Lowell's pulpit. Josiah seemed to be pressing for something, but Raymond had no idea what. His friend's eyes were intense, seemed to be burning, almost, though not with anger as much as with focus. Raymond realized Josiah believed there was something here to know. Reverend Lowell didn't appear to be hiding anything. There was no shame or embarrassment on his old face.

Raymond examined that face for a moment. Reverend Lowell had crops of violently white hair ringing his bald scalp, and intelligent blue eyes behind a nice pair of eyeglasses. He had only known the Reverend for a few weeks, but he liked the man, and trusted him. He wondered now what it was that Josiah thought he might know about the thing in the woods or about Sidney Seagram.

"I never knew about that, and it's hard to believe, though I believe you. But around that time there were several terrible things that happened not far from where we sit." He paused, as though he were recalling the events first in order to be sure of what he'd say. "There was a fire, first of all. I don't believe anyone was killed, I'm nearly certain no one was, but it destroyed several businesses in town, and one or two people were severely burned. I seem to remember one being a woman, but you'd have to verify that. I can't be quite sure." He stopped again, and now seemed to look past Josiah for a moment, though Raymond didn't see the man's eyes actually move.

"The other was a killing, a murder. A very strange one."

"A murder?" Raymond asked, incredulously. An accidental death he could imagine, and even a death at the hands of a bear or a pack of wolves, especially fifty years prior when the town would have been an even smaller collection of settlements on the edge of woods stretching for miles off towards the foothills of the Berkshire Mountains. But a murder, setting aside Hannibal Guthridge's crazed killing of his neighbor two days prior, seemed beyond belief to Raymond. He had only been in Sunbury for a little more than a month, but it was as uneventful and peaceable a town as he imagined existed in New England. Still, he supposed he had to allow for the fact that a murder could happen anywhere there are people.

"Yes, it was unusual to have something like that occur here. Still is, clearly. It was a spiritualist who had only been in Sunbury for a week or so. I remember him

Chapter 16

making a fair bit of noise in town, and I even saw him once, speaking to people in front of the Inn. He was remarkable to see, very animated in his affect, in the way he spoke and conjured up images with his hands." Reverend Lowell smiled in a way that seemed to Raymond to be an act of forgiveness towards his town. "He seemed to be pleading with people to take his nonsense seriously. I remember thinking he was persuasive, purely in his speech, I mean, and he succeeded in drumming up a bit of business for himself. His voice was a bit high-pitched, he had a very well-kept brown mustache, and he was wearing a green suit that day, with a very bright white shirt and a flower or a colorful handkerchief or something like that near his shirt pocket. He certainly left an impression." Reverend Lowell tapped his own left breast with his left hand, and gave a simple, melancholy smirk. He looked down for a moment.

"Someone stabbed him through the eye."

The Reverend looked away from them for a moment, and was silent, pensive about something. "I haven't thought about that in years. Many years." He looked back at Josiah, though as he continued to talk Raymond knew it was to both of them. "I believe he'd been holding one of his meetings at the Inn, and some of those who were there discovered him. The murderer was never caught, and I don't seem to remember anyone's name in town really being under much suspicion. After several months it was largely forgotten. Or at least any hope of punishing the guilty was."

He was silent again, but now he looked right at Josiah as though he were either confused or might have something else to say. Raymond was certainly confused himself, unsure of whether these old events had anything to do with what Sidney Seagram had discovered, unsure of why Reverend Lowell brought them up.

"It seems unlikely that these things aren't somehow related," Josiah said finally, in an even and nearly certain tone. Raymond was surprised.

"Why?" Raymond asked. "I don't understand how this man's murder fifty years ago has anything to do with whoever or whatever accosted you and dug up those graves." He sounded irritable, and he regretted it, but he was deeply tired and concerned about Rachel, and he also had the sense that he was wasting time now, very precious time needed to stop whatever the threat was.

"Two murders," Josiah said. "Both around times when graves were desecrated. I can't see that being chance, being unrelated." He sounded tired to Raymond now, but in truth it was resignation. Josiah was accepting something he hadn't wanted to.

Reverend Lowell nodded, and then smiled grimly and said, "And one other thing I hadn't thought of until now."

17

1843

Theodore looked down through the dark to see what he could of Marvin's form. There wasn't much he could discern. His dead partner was on his back, and his arms were out to either side. He could just make out the handle of his knife jutting out of Marvin's left eye at an angle, away from the house. Theodore looked for another four or five seconds, and then turned away from him towards the back of the house.

At first he had no thought to grab his knife. The idea of a future where he might be caught and tried and hanged was nowhere in his conscious mind. One thought overshadowed any other for the moment, and it involved walking south, away from the Inn and towards the woods. But he did retrieve it after a few seconds. Then, before he stood, he smirked and whispered the fifteenth verse of the fifty-fifth Psalm to himself and to Marvin's lifeless body. It was one of many texts of Scripture Theodore's father had had him commit to memory as a boy, and though he only understood the surface of its meaning, saying it seemed a profound sort of irony to him right then.

Theodore had seen it on the roof. He had smiled, and wondered, and the thought he was carrying with him now had germinated in his mind right then. If I had met Theodore McCabe as a young boy and told him that one day he would become infatuated with a monster, seek after it the way a young man would pursue a woman, he would have laughed or found the idea unintelligible. But the man who had just murdered Marvin Branson was a very different one from the Theodore McCabe his family cherished fond childhood memories of. Theodore McCabe had become a very different man in the last ten years, and a much more diabolical one in the last two. What happened this night would have not been so surprising to Marvin Branson.

The dark just a hundred yards from the Inn was impenetrable. Theodore couldn't see anything other than stars above his head and the faintest outline of a few trees in the flat land ahead of him. But he smiled, knowing from what he heard that this was the direction it had gone. He would find it.

18

1892

"Mrs. Tufts?"

Rachel's feet sounded abnormally loud. She wished more than anything she could be quieter. But the last of her quick eight steps put her in the front room, and there was Mrs. Tufts, looking out the window in the front of their house, peering into the dark outside. Rachel couldn't see her face, but she gathered the woman was intent and curious from how close it was to the glass. The gray streaks in her otherwise dark hair, pulled up tight above her head, shown clearly in the reflection made possible by the lamp to her left. But everything else was too blurry to make out.

"Mrs. Tufts, please put out the light," Rachel said a bit frantically, almost crying, and now the woman looked over to her right and saw Rachel, out of bed despite her injury, and instantly stood up and began to moan over the poor girl's obvious fright. But despite her natural skepticism concerning the emotions of young people, she put the out the light as requested and then shuffled quickly over to Rachel in the dark.

"I heard it, too, dear, but I don't expect there's anything that should frighten us." It was said without a speck of actual knowledge as to what had caused the sounds on the roof or who had fired what she already knew was a rifle, or as to what the earlier long, piercing sound had been, but it had the unexpected effect of landing where she'd intended it, right in Rachel's tired and frightened heart, and as her old, dry lips kissed the young girl's forehead Rachel was suddenly very much aware that she loved Mrs. Tufts. There it was, as true and inescapable as the color of her eyes or the fracture in her arm or the chip in the handle of the teacup she used each morning: The first woman she had come to love after her mother died.

Rachel began to cry, and she wasn't nearly as embarrassed by it as she would have expected had she known that would be her reaction to the woman's tenderness. Mrs. Tufts' neck or face smelled a bit like camphor, but the smell didn't bother her right now, and somehow Rachel began to associate it with the woman's help, her presence, her strength. She wasn't speaking at all, her chin was simply resting lightly on the back of Rachel's head, and there was something firm and hopeful about that and the stiffness of her arms now wrapped all the way around Rachel.

Rachel was frightened by what she'd seen out the window. There was nowhere to hide from what it was, or what it wasn't. It had been on the roof, and it was bigger than a man should be, and its eyes weren't a man's. She couldn't say it out loud, but the image was all she could think about for the moment. It had moved so swiftly to the right, away from the house, she

Chapter 18

thought, and she didn't think it was here now. But it had been here, and it had looked at her, and it had broken her arm last night. And there would be no way to defend herself against it if it came back, and not even Mrs. Tufts would be able to help with that. It had to be a foot taller than any man she had ever seen, and she guessed it was wider, stronger, too. She wasn't unsettled yet about what to call it or what it might mean that such a thing existed in the world, she was simply terrified that the next time she turned around she would see its eyes inside the house. She would hear what she knew just had to be a hoarse, thick breathing, and smell something from far outside in a wilder place, something that would have only biting and killing and eating in its purposes.

They both heard the sounds of people running, two or three, it seemed, just outside the house, now, but neither one looked towards the front windows or the door. Rachel jumped just a bit, but then she dug her fingernails in to Mrs. Tufts' white blouse and her fleshy right arm just underneath it, and Mrs. Tufts didn't move a hair's breadth.

In that moment of clutching Mrs. Tufts, Rachel drowned in the sense that this had all happened before. She had no delusions that this day, these actual moments of terror at the monster outside the window and the fire in her arm and the smell of the camphor, had occurred in a past life or even yesterday. She knew better than such things. But it was the feeling of fear leaving her and an awareness that what was happening next was supposed to happen, was falling into place just so as it was all intended, that she might even know how this week or this night would finish up. Her breathing slowed a bit, and her brow furrowed over her closed eyes. She pulled her mind back to her prayers and asked God to help her be obedient and brave. She wound her way back to her pleadings with God and God's dealings with her just before she'd looked out the window in her bedroom.

There were several loud words uttered outside the front door that she couldn't make out, mostly, it seemed to her, because her face was tight up against Mrs. Tufts, but then the door opened and she knew it was her father, and she was right.

"Rachel!" She heard two quick and loud footsteps and then felt herself being pulled from Mrs. Tufts, and the pain in her arm was so blinding she thought she might faint, and she screamed. But her father became tender then, remembering the pain she was in, and when she opened her eyes, she saw his eyes looking back at her. They were smiling eyes, now, and she was surprised by that. His face was wet with sweat, and he smelled like sweat and leather and the outside air, and she actually smiled back at him, merely because of how much she loved him. And then she told him what she had seen outside, and he told her what Dr. Hall

Chapter 18

thought, and then Josiah Hall came into the house and nodded at both women, and once the lamp had been relit, he told them both himself.

* * *

Reverend Lowell was a flavorful man. The jagged tufts of gray-white hair that sprung up around his head but never creeped up above the scalp, the sharpness of his eyes despite his glasses, and the fact he was thin but with big hands that gave the impression he was once much wider and more muscular, these features made him memorable even at a glance. He never used a cane, but he should have. His lower back and knees hurt him often, and at times when he stood, he could barely breathe or speak for a few seconds because of the pain. But he had an internal resistance to anything that might be gaudy, and so he merely walked slowly and stood up more slowly, unaided. He felt cold down to his bones, now, and this night he was quite sure some of it was an uneasiness about what was happening, but some of it was also just growing old, being near to the end of his earthly walk

  He wasn't sure whether what he'd told Dr. Hall and Mr. Stanton would matter much. But he did believe that something beyond a normal human evil was acting upon his town. He did feel it was his town, as much as he supposed a man could. He'd been here since he was a boy, over sixty years now. His mother and father had come from Indiana, from a hillside glen with a cabin nested in it that now felt like another life. He couldn't remember anything about the inside of the cabin. His whole life seemed to be in Sunbury. He had shepherded three generations of several families by now. It was his as much as any place could be any man's and it was the same for Hannibal Guthridge, he thought. Hannibal sitting in Noel's office, waiting for his trial and his hanging. The thought of the old neighbor, even an ornery one like Hannibal, sitting alone in a dark room waiting for the judge and for his death, owed to him for murder but still seeming somehow tragic, it left a sharp point of angst in Reverend Lowell's chest. A murder here in his town, and then an execution, and it being just a ripple in some stronger current, it made him wish he could be younger and more alive than he was. If there was a demonic monster of some sort out in those woods, sneaking into town to hurt folks and somehow make them crazier and more base and wicked, there wasn't much he felt he could do about it. His bones were as old as the walls of his church, creaking just as much and no doubt fading and splintering in their own right, too. He wouldn't be much help in the fight against this thing, if a fight was what was called for. And that hurt him. It worried him. For the first time he'd hoped, tonight, that he died soon.

Chapter 18

The small room at the back of the church building where he kept his books and a small table and chair was comfortable for him in moments like this. At least it had been for the several he'd had in the past. And as he came to the table and grabbed his Bible, he felt a drop better than when he'd been in the mostly dark sanctuary. He knelt down in front of the chair, put his head on the cover of the Bible and closed his eyes. He needed his God to help his town, his people, now. He had no way himself to do anything, but something would have to be done if any of what he feared were true. Even if there was nothing more than a bear or a drunk roaming around at night in the village, Ed Aimes' murder was a real event, a strain on the cables that held Sunbury together. And someone had stolen two bodies out of the cemetery, two bodies of folks who were still missed and still being grieved. Sunbury was unsettled, and he loved her, and that was why his eyes were clenched so tight now that sparks were fluttering in the night that hung in between them and the cover of his Bible.

"Almighty God, what is out there?"

He was surprised to hear himself ask a question like that, but he felt no remorse about it, and decided that was probably proper. There was nothing sinful about wondering if something evil lived in the woods. But he resolved not to let the prayer die in that question.

Nephilim

"Lord, you love these sheep more than I do. Much more. I don't love them as I should, but I do love them. I'm frightened, Father." His face felt hot, now, though his bones and his chest and his hands and feet still felt cold. He wondered if something might be wrong with his heart, but he left that fear aside and pleaded with God for Mrs. Steatham and the Klines and the Tufts and the Jansens and the Stantons and Dr. Hall and all of them.

"Whatever happens, Lord, I ask you to protect them. Keep them safe in your care. They know so little of you, because my preaching and my ministry are so weak and small and insufficient. I wish I could have been a better man, Father. I am sorry for what I haven't been." His thoughts wandered over his failures, and his face became even hotter, and he felt a stream of tears begin in both eyes.

A mile away in thick darkness, the monster stopped running. It wasn't sure why.

* * *

Reverend Lowell decided he couldn't wait to go talk with Jason Bloomfield. Jason was a good, if quiet, member of their church, and Reverend Lowell accounted for the fact that he would have some influence over the man he could put to good use. He didn't believe Jason would remember much about the

Chapter 18

murdered man who'd stayed in his parents' Inn, he'd only been a boy when it had happened. But he had good reason to believe that, even if nothing else, some object would have been left behind. Murders leave marks on folks and on towns. It was the only reason, he now figured as he thought back on talking with Dr. Hall and Mr. Stanton, that he had remembered all he did about the man's dress and manner and those days he'd been in Sunbury fifty years prior. Finding out a man has been murdered locks everything you know about him and everything that happened around him in place in your memory, leaves it fortified against passing time and old age. Harold and June would have talked about what happened outside their Inn in the years after, or they would have kept something that belonged to the man, or there would be some scrap of paper or picture or something they held on to. Reverend Lowell sunk his frail upper body into his grey wool overcoat a bit more, knowing that it was still quite warm to everyone outside his own skin but that his own bones and blood would always be a touch chill until Providence blessed him with healing or he went home. The back of his neck was tickled a bit by the collar, and for some reason he smirked a bit at that and quickened his step. The Inn was only a hundred yards away now. He'd be warmer once Jason let him inside.

Jason Bloomfield did indeed take his pastor inside right away, and in his quiet way he was excited and happy to see him despite the hour of night. He offered a chair in the front room, near a window where one of the shrieking old women had sat during Marvin Branson's last night of telling lies to make a living. Something about the chair felt odd to Reverend Lowell, but Jason couldn't tell. That was of course a strength of an old man who had been visiting the homes of his flock for only a shade less than a lifetime, now. The chair felt unbalanced in its seat somehow, but he silently tightened up his lower back a bit, then loosened it, and he felt the pain drip away for a few seconds. *It's all right. I'll be walking again soon.*

"Jason, how are you?"

Jason nodded and raised his lips thoughtfully, then smoothed back his thinning silver hair. "Mighty well," he answered truthfully, though without the smile one might expect. His was a quiet face, tired but kind, and Reverend Lowell was pleased to ponder for a moment in the quiet after "well" that he couldn't remember a single instance of Jason Bloomfield complaining. Certainly, it must have happened, but he had the memory of a good pastor, which is to say he could recall the frailties and needs and crises of everyone who had been a member of his church for more than one summer, and he couldn't remember any murmuring or strife from Jason's lips in the man's entire grown life.

Chapter 18

"Could I ask you something about an old matter?" Reverend Lowell said with the care and smile of a man who clearly intended to proceed only if invited. Jason nodded plainly and then looked down at the table, a habit he'd carried for all of his fifty-seven years.

"Do you remember the fellow who was murdered here when you were a boy?"

Jason nodded the same way, without any reticence or even curiosity. Someone who didn't know him would almost certainly have been put off at such a businesslike demeanor to inquiries about something so dark, but Reverend Lowell did know him and so still smiled warmly and went on. "I don't doubt this will sound strange, Jason, but I wonder if your parents ever said anything about him, his being killed and all." He paused only for a second, and only because he still wasn't quite sure himself. "I'm afraid that what happened in the cemetery and with Hannibal Guthridge yesterday might have something to do with what happened to that man."

Jason furrowed his brow, obviously confused, but then he stood up without saying anything and shuffled back towards the kitchen of what had once been the Inn. Jason's left foot had been injured about ten years after his mother died and left him the property, and he'd limped severely ever since. He had some help in a young farmhand named Jesse, who stayed in a small room Jason had constructed in the barn he'd built shortly after converting the Inn into a farm, but even held back by his slow gait he still loved to be outdoors and in the dirt and sun and rain and wind. He'd always been that way.

"They kept what he'd had in the room. No one ever came to ask after it." Jason turned back, now standing at the large bureau in the kitchen where his mother had once kept all her best plates and bowls. Reverend Lowell could see he was preparing to open it, but he had stopped with a thought. "Did you know he was staying here at the time?"

Reverend Lowell nodded, but then caught himself as he realized he hadn't quite remembered that. "I suppose I assumed it, but come to think of it I'm not sure I did know that for certain." He squinted and thought back for a moment, and then continued. "I remember seeing him out front here," he nodded to his left towards the front of the house, "speaking with a few folks about his presentation, but I don't suppose I did actually know that he was staying here." He had raised his white eyebrows above his glasses when he'd said "presentation," and Jason had actually smiled a bit at that.

"I never heard much about the man," Jason said, "but it troubled father and mother. They were afraid whoever had killed him would come back for these." Jason turned back to the cabinet and bent down to take

Chapter 18

out Marvin Branson's trunk, his overcoat, and his satchel.

* * *

Josiah Hall started with what he was sure the thing wasn't.

"I don't believe it is man." Something about the way he said that, as though he were describing another species of being rather than merely saying whatever had broken her arm wasn't a person, made Rachel wince. She thought of the eyes again, and she was as terrified as she had ever been.

"The first reason is that it dug out Mr. Steatham and Mrs. Atwood in one night without anyone noticing, which seems unlikely if it had been a man or men using tools, or if it had taken hours, as one would expect for it to have taken men to unearth them. The second is that there were no wagon tracks or wheelbarrow tracks in the grass, suggesting Mr. Steatham and Mrs. Atwood were carried out by hand, and it does not seem to me likely a typical grave robber or hooligan would have done such a thing. Then there is the horse, a valuable animal not stolen but slaughtered, and fairly savagely I might add, and merely left out in the open. Finally, there are the marks on the tree."

Here he let Raymond explain what they had found in the woods the day prior. Rachel didn't tell her father or Dr. Hall about the carving she had found in the tree on their own property, but she wasn't at all sure why she didn't.

"The creature dragged me quickly towards the forest, and both that and its apparent obsession with the recently deceased, and particularly recently deceased who died of sickness, confirms for me we are not dealing with an animal intelligence." Josiah looked at Mrs. Tufts, now, and while he was scared himself, she thought of him as only tired. His eyes had violet circles under them she could make out now that the lamp had been re-lit, and his face was unshaven. She wondered what had compelled him to this interest in the thing.

"I do not have a name to for it, but I'm of the mind we're dealing with a material creature touched by immaterial forces. It is large, probably seven feet tall, or so, and it is much more quick and stronger than any man. It is at least fifty years old, and it could be far older. And I believe its evil intent is caused by an affinity with the Devil, or with the demonic generally." He stopped speaking for a second, looking back at Raymond, who had stepped away from Mrs. Tufts and Rachel instinctively as Josiah had begun speaking. He knew she needed Mrs. Tufts at the moment, and he had some sense of the reason why.

"What do we do, Dr. Hall?" Mrs. Tufts asked, with no wavering in her voice, though she felt terror in her heart.

Chapter 18

"I think we must find it and disable it," he said plainly, though lowering the volume of his speech at the last few words, as though he feared the creature might hear him. "I haven't yet spoken with Noel Flagler about this, but that is our next step. And I believe we can find it in the woods, being a large creature and with its intent apparently being to hunt us."

"I wish you were more mad or more sane, Josiah," said Mrs. Tufts, and she meant to smile but forgot. Josiah did it for her, and even Raymond smirked a bit from where he stood over towards the door.

"I don't know how, ladies," he said, and nodded and looked at Rachel, who was standing almost straight now, leaning just slightly on Mrs. Tufts to her left. "I didn't think such things happened in our day. But I do believe it's some sort of giant, and its hatred of us and its interest in sickness and death have me of the mind that its portion is with Hell. If it's made of flesh and bone, I venture it can be killed, or at least disabled. That's the measure we intend to take." He looked over at Raymond, who nodded, but who then looked at the floor of his own house as though he were ashamed of something.

"Father?" Rachel said.

He looked up without speaking but raised his eyebrows as a granting of permission for whatever she would ask. And whatever it was, she asked without words.

Nephilim

    His eyes became wet, and he dropped his shoulders, and he put his left hand to his forehead. Rachel wondered what was happening to him right then, whether the fear of her being hurt was still working on him or something else had happened in all of this that he and Dr. Hall hadn't yet said. But she left Mrs. Tufts' shoulder. She walked over to her father and put her arms around him, clasping her hands just beneath his shoulders, and rested her head on his chest. He cried, and she was sorry that he was ashamed of something, and wished she could discern what it was, but in the glow of the lamp there in their house she let him be silent. Mrs. Tufts looked away, and before long Dr. Hall did, too.

19

1843

Theodore stopped walking when he heard it breathing. If it were an animal, it knew you were there long before you heard it breathing. But it wasn't an animal. He knew that.

He heard the quick panting on the other side of a tall bluff of limestone that was covered in dirt and moss. He was terrified, now that he knew the thing he had seen on the roof of the Inn, a creature large enough and undoubtedly strong enough to rip his arms and head from his body the way he himself might uproot a dandelion, was just on the other side of this rock.

Suddenly, Theodore's drunken fascination seemed distant. As the panting slowed and shifted a bit, as though the creature had taken a large step to its right, he felt only fear of pain and death. He hadn't felt that sort of fear in years. It surprised him that his feet seemed frozen to the soil and sparse grass beneath him. He had forgotten how fear could paralyze you. The hand that had held the knife still bearing blood from Marvin Branson's orbital was flexing and loosening repeatedly, and he felt the coolness of air against his sweaty palm. What would it feel like to have your arms torn from your body?

He took one slow step away from the rock, and then heard what he knew had to be running. And so he turned and began to run with a speed he didn't know he had. His feet only hit the ground four times before he felt himself flying through dark air and catching glimpses of the forest floor underneath him. Then there was a sudden stabbing pain in his head and neck, and he tried to scream. He couldn't. And then he felt himself in the air again.

20

1892

"Will you wait until morning?" Mrs. Tufts asked.

"No," Raymond answered, and even as he did, Josiah was shaking his own head.

"Take your hat off, Dr. Hall," Mrs. Tufts said, and there was only a wisp of humor in it as she said it. She was mostly annoyed with these two men and afraid that more people, perhaps even she and Rachel, would die tonight. "We're in a home. Mr. Stanton's home, to be precise. And Mr. Stanton's daughter has been frightened quite badly. You can at least present yourself as a gentleman."

Josiah smiled and removed his hat.

Raymond looked back at his daughter, and she gazed at him for a moment before looking up at the ceiling. "I saw it," she said, and no one spoke for several seconds.

"Where?" Josiah and Raymond had both asked at about the same instant.

"Outside the window in my bedroom. It had been on the roof."

Raymond looked over at Josiah, but Dr. Hall was still staring at Rachel. He was wondering something, and Mrs. Tufts registered it. But then she pulled Rachel closer to her. Raymond looked back at his daughter and wished he had never brought her to Sunbury. Rachel's brown hair looked dark with only the one lamp on the other side of their front room lit and in the shadow of Mrs. Tufts. Somehow that made her look older to him, but then he took in her eyes, and she was still his young daughter. For a time, at least. Green and scared and still somehow hopeful, trusting that her father and Dr. Hall and Noel Flagler and the other men involved would sort it out. He wanted to tell her they up were up to it, but his words were caught in his throat and heart.

"Did it see you?"

There was a question underneath Dr. Hall's question. Rachel could tell that, despite being only sixteen years old. But she simply said, "I think so," and left whether or not there was something else she needed to know with Dr. Hall. She wasn't sure whether she wanted to know, anyway.

"What does that mean?" Raymond asked Dr. Hall.

"I believe the rifle shot alarmed it and sent it running for the woods. But I'm afraid we need to find it quickly. And if we don't, we'll need to have men outside this house, at least during the night."

"Why?" Raymond asked, narrowing his eyes. "Why my house?"

Josiah was thinking of the hairpin Noel had retrieved from the deep den in the woods, and of the creature's presence outside this house on consecutive

Chapter 20

nights, and of something more difficult for him to put into words. "I suspect it's after Rachel."

* * *

Reverend Lowell opened the satchel, having received Jason Bloomfield's permission to do so. He supposed Jason had as much right as anyone alive to allow it, and so he grounded any remorse he had and nervously stretched his fingers inside the bag. There was a handkerchief, a pair of eyeglasses, and two small books. He pulled both of the books out and set them on the table. It had been quite a while since he had held any books this old.

The smaller of the two had a dark green fabric cover and it appeared to be less than fifty pages. He picked it up in his left hand and gently opened it with his right. He loosened his grip on the cover when he saw how brittle and stiff the pages were, but he still turned three of them. It appeared to be day-to-day notes from the man, most particularly travel details and remarks. "8:15 train to Stoveport." "Send letter to M.C. once in Amherst." Reverend Lowell closed that book and set it on the table. He would look more at it later, assuming Jason let him take it home.

The second book was clearly a published volume, red-brown leather binding and numbering over 200 pages in length. At first glance he thought it might be a religious work, based chiefly on the seriousness of the binding. But when he turned it over and saw the title he squinted and clenched his teeth. He wasn't sure until now that such a thing was what he'd expected to find.

* * *

Noel and Joe had crossed into the woods within ten minutes of setting out. Neither was particularly scared yet, and that had as much to do with their familiarity with the woods as with any cultivated courage. Both had hunted more times than they could count under these very trees, and both had been in the woods at night. They knew they were chasing something big and harmful, but they had confidence in their aptitude to catch or kill a large creature out here.

Noel listened for Joe's dog, carefully waiting for the moment when it stopped moving and perked up as though it had smelled or heard something that arrested its attention. So far it was obediently sniffing the grass and tree trunks around them at Joe's side as they stepped over the light spring undergrowth. They were walking at a slow pace, but not with as much caution as Josiah would have.

Even with almost no clouds, the moonlight and starlight couldn't fight their way through the healthy blanket of leaves overhead, and so once the edge of the forest was a good way behind them, the men were

Chapter 20

almost blind. Joe had a kerosene lamp with him, but Noel wanted to wait until they had no other choice but to light it, and he still hoped they weren't far enough away from the creature for the dog to miss the scent if they had a bit of good fortune and walked thoughtfully. He tapped Joe's arm and then pulled it towards the southwest. A few hundred paces in that direction from where they stood now there was a streambed. Neither of them could see it, but Joe knew instinctively that was what Noel was headed for and walked with him without so much as a nod in agreement.

The dead leaves and undergrowth crumbled and cracked under their boots in the darkness as they tread slowly towards the streambed. After a few steps, the dog barked and backed up. Noel felt a rush of air and heard what he at first thought was the rustling of the trees above him. But then with squinted eyes and by stretching out his hand he was able to discern that Joe was gone. The dog began to bark again and wouldn't stop. Noel felt his heart beat faster, and despite knowing in a deep place what had happened, he said Joe's name in something between a whisper and a yell, scratchy and hoarse sounding.

"Joe?"

The dog yelped and then was silent.

* * *

Nephilim

Hannibal had already scratched his left forearm to the point of blood, but the itching had only gotten worse. He bit into his lower lip now, closed his eyes, and wondered whether there was a way to kill himself that he could tolerate.

He'd been angry for what seemed to him to be a month. The room where Noel was keeping him was about the size of his bedroom, but it had no window, and although his bedroom had no window, either, that fact had offended him. Everything was offending him right now. The burning in his left arm, the hot, vibrating itching, it was all he could think about when it got bad. It would dull every so often, and then he could consider the hot, stagnant office where he was waiting for the judge and his subsequent hanging, and that Ed Aimes had gotten off too easily, considering his boys were still alive, and that he would give almost anything to kill everyone in this town slowly. Noel first, then Ed Aimes' sons, then the girl, the brunette Stanton girl with the skin that reminded him of the sunset for some reason. His hatred for her was a thing he didn't examine, he simply drank it down and waited for it to push him to something. As he savored all such thoughts his anger became more rank and painful, and he became less able to escape it even long enough to nap.

The something was coming, though Hannibal no longer had the sort of mind needed to be aware of it.

Chapter 20

His head and heart had warped the morning he chopped off Ed Aimes' hand, and he had never had even a sense that the monster was any part of it. But Hannibal was now a man of violence and gnawed pride and hate, and while he was uncomfortable with the open wound he'd created on his own arm, he thought as much about his health and when and how he would die approximately as much as a coyote did. He stood up in the little room, looked at the deadbolt lock on the door, and decided that when Bill Kline came in to give him his meal, he would choke him or crush his head in the door and then go kill Aimes' sons. Rats. Dirty, loud, odious, grimy, worthless little rats. He would rip out their tongues and crush their faces under his boots and laugh at their corpses before burning them in their house. He smiled for the first time that day, and sat down, and his heart seemed to slow and even his arm stopped itching and burning. He didn't hear several minutes later when the door in the outer office bust open. He had finally drifted off to a calm sleep.

Out in the office the thing stood, breathing like a grizzly, with a heave and a grunt that felt like there was a power under its skin that could flatten you without any effort. It stepped once, and there was a great creak under the floorboards of the office Noel kept in town, then it stopped. There was a light behind it, clinking through the bottom panes of glass in the front window like a moving star. It shone first on the boards just behind it. Then on its right foot. Light was always a reason to stop, to look. It turned, and there was a swifter movement to the light now, and it had become brighter. It was moving first one way, away from it, then quickly back towards it, and now the light was brighter and blinding. It stepped away, into the shadows of the room, and heard two voices outside. Human voices.

"What happened to the door?"

"I'll be damned if I know. What done that?"

It waited in the shadow on the other side of the doorframe, waiting for the voices to come close enough.

"We better make sure he's all right."

"I don't know, Bill. What if he's the one who done it? And he's in there waiting on us?"

"I don't believe Hannibal Guthridge has the strength to rip that door off like that. I'm supposing something else happened, and whatever it was could have happened to him, too. I was charged to look after him, and that's what I intend to do."

It heard the step up onto the wood just outside the room. It waited for a second one to follow. Then, with no thought other than its hate, it came out of the darkness and grabbed the first man. He screamed, and then his voice was far off, and the second man began to run. It reached him in two steps that seemed impossible to the man, and then it made him quiet by taking his life

Chapter 20

from him and planted its foot in the blood already turning the dust of the street into paste just to the right of what remained of the man's head. It considered finding the first man, the one it had cast into the deep darkness, but then turned back to what it had come for.

Hannibal was still asleep. He didn't wake up until the locked door he had expected Bill Kline to come through was ripped off its frame and flung against the wall of the little office outside his room. He thought it was a nightmare, at first, and then he thought he was awake but in the middle of a tornado. Finally he saw just enough of the thing outside the hole where there used to be a door to understand he was about to die.

His arm itched again.

* * *

Raymond believed Josiah, not only because he trusted the man implicitly, but also because in some corner of his mind he, too, suspected the thing was after his daughter. It was a hard, thick shadow he couldn't quite understand, but it was more than simple fear. He looked at Rachel and felt the back of his neck begin to sweat, and decided that he had no idea how to kill a monster. He had the thought several times throughout the night that it all had to be a dream, but knowing that it wasn't and that this thing had to be killed gave him all the will he needed to rely on Josiah and Noel Flagler.

There would be no other way to catch and do away with whatever this thing was. Josiah was looking out the front door of Raymond's house, now, and Raymond found it difficult to do the thing he wanted to do before leaving.

Rachel was standing to Mrs. Tufts' right, her arms behind her back. She was swaying gently, her head was angled down and to her right. Raymond studied her hair for a moment. It was brown in a lively way, even here in a room still shadowed, and it struck him that she was not yet a full-grown woman, but yet no longer a girl. He spent a few seconds wondering why it was so hard to speak, and why he couldn't lift his left foot and then his right and walk over to her. There was something he was ashamed of, something much deeper than a mere failure as a father. He had many failures, and he had generally confessed them to Rachel, but right now in the front room of their house he felt ashamed to be her father, ashamed to be alive, and ashamed to be holding a rifle as though there were anything meaningful he could do with it. This was no cougar they were after.

It was surprising to him that he did walk over to her and kiss her cheek, and almost as surprising to him that she instantly began to cry. But he embraced her, knowing in his bones and muscles what he was called to do even if in his wits he did not, and Mrs. Tufts turned away for the second time that night. Rachel's sobbing continued for several moments, but when she was

Chapter 20

done, she looked up at Raymond and smiled, and he smiled back merely because she was beautiful and the affection he had for her was much deeper than the fear he felt presently. They didn't say anything, but when he turned to Josiah, Rachel began humming something softly, and Raymond listened to it and loved her.

"I believe Noel has gone into the woods," Josiah said, still looking out the Stanton's front door and into the night. "I'm not sure whether we'll be able to find him if he has, but we'd do best to try." Raymond didn't answer in any way other than to put the barrel of his rifle on his left shoulder and step up just behind Josiah. Josiah heard him behind him and took it as answer enough. They both stepped out onto the front of Raymond's property and turned immediately south, walking quickly towards the trees they couldn't see in the distance.

* * *

There was only one place Rachel could think to be, and that was there in the front room with their little table in front of her, and Mrs. Tufts at her side, and the lantern shedding just enough light on their edition of *The Pilgrim's Progress* for her to keep her eyes dreamily on the illustration of Giant Despair. She wondered at the fact that she had opened it to that page. *Gigantes* was the word in the Latin Bible, the Vulgate, she remembered.

Nephilim

She had cold chills racing down her back at the thought of opening to the page she had, but she reasoned that God was in control of the slightest moves of our fingers and the falling of paper and the placement of illustrations in books and that she had best think of the story if she couldn't read it. She lay her head on Mrs. Tufts' left shoulder, and while her friend wasn't asleep, her eyes were closed, and she was tired enough to let Rachel do it without asking any questions about her state or whether she wanted something to eat or drink. Rachel was grateful for that, and for the fact that she could see enough of the words on the page to draw herself into the part of the story there that was open, of Giant Despair and Doubting Castle and Christian and his companion, Hopeful. And she began to feel a bit firmer and aware of God's rule in what was surely the most fantastic night of her life. They would have to kill some sort of beast that was stalking her, and others, but the Lord was still hers, and the world was still His.

Mrs. Tufts fell asleep before it opened the front door. And oddly enough she stayed asleep. It had to stoop to come into the house, dark now after Rachel had put out the lamp. The only light was from stars and moon, and that was only just enough to see that it had arms and legs like a man, and just enough to glitter off its eyes that were larger and had only the black pupils she'd seen outside her window. Together they formed the most terrifying thing Rachel had ever seen, and her

Chapter 20

heart seemed to be down in her knees as she whispered something to herself without any idea of what it was or why. It stared at her for several seconds, then it began speaking to her in Latin, in a whisper that sounded farther away than it was.

She knew enough Latin to understand that it had asked her if she knew its name, and for some reason she began to feel a better handle on her mind and her mouth, and she answered it "No." Mrs. Tufts stirred at that, but she didn't wake up. The thing hadn't moved at all since stepping fully into the house. If it did, the floorboards would creak, or groan, and Mrs. Tufts would sit up straight and might startle it. Rachel felt she had to keep it still and calm and where it was. She looked at the man shape of it as she waited for it to speak again. She knew it wasn't a man. She knew that from its eyes and its height and the dark shape of its body that was much too large for a man, but she could make out a hand at its right side before putting her gaze back on its eyes. She had trouble convincing herself that she wasn't somehow talking to the corpse of a giant man who had crawled out of his grave.

"What are you?" She whispered it in Latin that she had learned from two teachers, mostly from Mr. Hargrave, who had thinning red hair and a mustache that he waxed at the tips. She thought of Mr. Hargrave, and of cases and verb endings, and she begged God for this to be a dream, for her to not actually be talking to a demon creature in a dead language.

Its eyes closed. She waited for an answer, or for it to lunge at her, but neither happened. Then she felt herself asking the question she most cared about.

"What do you want?"

You.

It had a bit of the thing's actual voice, not the mere whisper it had spoken with first. Its voice was deep, but not as deep as she'd imagined. And it had a tone to it that seemed musical, but in a minor key.

"Why?"

Him.

Here it moved, and she seemed to be watching herself bracing for death, but it didn't strike her. It was still there where it had been, and she heard a thud near her feet. She looked down, but the moonlight wasn't reaching the floor, and she couldn't see exactly where the object had landed and couldn't bring herself to reach for it.

"How old are you?" she asked. She was stalling, now. Disbelief and trying to push off the moment of attack. That was what controlled her speech.

The eyes narrowed. *I was here when the world was wet.*

Is that what it said? *Wet?* Yes, she decided.

She prayed silently and without breathing, and something subtle changed inside. She was still afraid of

Chapter 20

the pain this creature could inflict on her, still feeling as though she was floating above a woman who was about to be ripped apart rather than being that woman herself, but she also seemed to see more clearly what it was to be murdered and that God was still her God and this thing couldn't change what mattered most.

She hadn't realized that she'd said any more words out loud, but she heard it whisper again in response, and this time Mrs. Tufts jerked awake. But before she did, Rachel heard the words. *I hate him.* Then she heard rustling outside in the grass in front of her house, and the thing rushed back out, and she heard a shot that made both her and Mrs. Tufts jump. It broke like a single crack of thunder, then she heard a long, angry, loud cry, and it broke off so suddenly, with no fading out like there would have been had it ended naturally, that she knew it had died. For a few seconds she was so sure it was the creature that had screamed and been shot dead that she stood up. But then she saw its dark shape run off to the south, away from her house. Her heart fell, her hands felt icy, and her arm throbbed with new pain as her breath quickened and she felt like fainting. Outside someone was dead, but she couldn't move, and so she started praying again. Then she saw Mrs. Tufts turn on the lamp and head towards the door.

21
1843

Theodore was surprised that he was not dead. The pain in his head and neck and left shoulder were sharp enough to make him scream if he'd had the power to, and he wondered for a few seconds if this perhaps was death, or something like death. He smelled old leaves, felt their crunch under his right cheek and smelled dirt, and while he couldn't see much of anything he knew his eyes were functioning well enough that he could make out the shape of a single tree a foot or two in front of his face. He was on the ground, on his belly.

He tried to stand and found he couldn't feel his legs. He felt as though he would lose consciousness, but he willed himself to stay awake and listen. The thing hadn't killed him yet, but if he didn't hide from it, it certainly would soon. He held his breath for three or four seconds, then realized he would pass out if he didn't breathe and did his best to do it quietly as he listened for the heavy steps or grunts of what he knew was a creature large enough to toss him through the air the way he might toss a housecat. His eyes frantically moved about the scene in mimicking his listening, but he still couldn't see anything worth seeing. Then, he heard what fear at first made him believe was only a few feet away but, after a moment he was able to conclude was much further off. It was the snap of what he

Chapter 21

imagined was a stick. Then the rustling of some leaves or foliage. Then there was a braying, animal sound. It wasn't quite the sound from earlier, on the roof, when he'd first seen it. It was its voice. He knew that, and he knew it would be coming back for him. He tried to move his legs once more, but found that he couldn't feel them. He knew that was potentially catastrophic, but he found some surprising physical strength and will in his being and body that took over and enabled him to pull himself into a position leaning on his right hand. His neck felt warm and there was lightning shooting up and down it now that he had shifted positions. Then he heard what he'd dreaded, and his heart thudded faster than he imagined it was ever intended to, and the pain in his neck almost made him cry out as blood flew furiously through his body.

He heard the unimaginably fast rustling of leaves and undergrowth that he knew meant the thing was running. And they were growing louder, which meant it was running towards him. He pictured the giant with the dead eyes and evening sky color he'd seen on the roof of the inn turning abruptly and pounding the earth with its feet in cruel intent towards him. He imagined that it ran like a deranged dog. He gave a whimper as he felt the world get more distant and blurry, as though he were somewhere else in a room with dry furniture and a fire making simple sounds nearby. There was no regret for what he'd done to Marvin, for anything he'd ever done. There was a panicky desire to stay alive and, concurrent with that, a resigned feeling that this was all happening to someone else and would be over soon. The pounding of earth under its feet was closer now, and it seemed to him that he could even hear air whirring about the creature as it ran.

Some part of him used his left arm to find the tree in front of him, and the same part pulled his agonized body forward, dragging his dead legs over the dirt. There might be some place he could hide, and as he thought this, he heard the sounds stop. He stopped moving himself. Was it right in front of him? He gave himself only a few seconds to think and then pulled himself once more in the direction of the tree and whatever lay beyond. Then he felt blinding pain on the left side of his head, and he screamed.

22

1892

Mrs. Tufts screamed, but even at that Rachel found it difficult to move.

She was standing, and she knew the thing it had thrown to her, whatever it was, was still at her feet and that she must look at it. She knew something horrible had happened outside, and that the monster would return. All of these facts were webbed in front of her. She took stock of each. She hadn't lost the ability to reason about what they meant, that she and Mrs. Tufts and her father and others might be killed by this thing or haunted by it forever, and that she had a responsibility to see what was wrong in front of their house and perhaps help. But the muscles in her legs seemed to be gone, and her eyes didn't respond to her directions to them. She felt as though she had been swimming, when all of a sudden the ocean around her had frozen solid and she was trapped forever in what might as well be her coffin.

Mrs. Tufts' running out into the night is what gave Rachel the freedom to move, though she did so slowly. She felt a kind of thickness in the air, and so her steps were much more gradual than she would have expected in a moment of fear and blood and gunshot. She crossed the threshold of their front door and stepped out onto the cool night grass a full thirty

Nephilim

seconds after Mrs. Tufts had run out. Now she could see under the faint starlight and the moon and the glimmer of the lone lamp across the road that she was gone. But there was a still form in the grass a few feet in front of her, and she covered her mouth and began to cry. Once the crying started, she found she couldn't stop, and without any thought she could discern, she fell into a sitting position just in front of their front door. Her head went down, and her fingers went up to her hair, and there they dug into the skin of her head and her crying became violent.

She prayed again. She asked God to make this all end, whatever it was, and she asked Him to keep them safe, her and her father and Mrs. Tufts, and she asked Him to make what she thought was in front of her not be that.

Please, God, please our Great Redeemer, please let it not be the dead body of a person.

She begged God that it not be the lifeless body of someone who was real and who she knew and who had a face and hair and eyes that wouldn't move when she looked down at them. She heard Mrs. Tufts calling to her after a moment of that prayer, and she forced herself to look up with a reserve of strength she'd had almost no experience with. When the light from Mrs. Tufts' lamp scattered across the grass as she held it in her left hand, holding up her dress with her right, Rachel saw that it was Noel Flagler on the ground, and

Chapter 22

that his head was bent too far back, and that he was dead, and she began to cry more fiercely. But she forced herself to keep her head up this time, and she began to be very worried about her father.

* * *

The woods were even darker than Raymond had feared they would be. They smelled wet despite the fact that it hadn't rained. They stepped on soft soil, not yet hardened by a full summer, and Raymond wondered whether the creature might even now be close by. Josiah held a small lantern near his chest, away from his body just enough to cast light for a few paces in front of them.

He ventured the chance to talk.

"Why do you think it dug up the graves?"

He expected Josiah to silence him, but he didn't. He took that to mean Josiah believed they weren't near it yet. He was scanning the darkness for something, Noel Flagler's lantern, perhaps, or a tell that the creature had been nearby, but something must have made him believe that it wasn't presently near them since he answered.

"I suspect it loves death," he said, without any flourish or emotion. Josiah was in fact disgusted at the vague impressions he had of the monster's purposes and origins, but it was a feature of his that he spoke even the most fantastic things with little tone worth remembering.

They kept walking, and after ten or twenty steps, seeing nothing but waves of ancient tree trunks and thick night and forest floor, he continued.

"I think it adores death the way you or I adore an embrace or an anniversary or a good story." The way he included himself in the love of such things was humorous to Raymond. He smiled at the thought of Dr. Josiah Hall being given a kiss on the cheek by an affectionate female relative, looking as though he were suffering from dysentery as the assault lingered. Raymond savored that grin in the dark. It was the first he'd had in a while, and the last he expected in a while.

Raymond was going to ask what he thought it would do next when they heard a rifle shot behind them. Both men turned quickly towards Sunbury. Raymond took three steps in the direction of the town, but they were too far into the woods now to see anything back that way.

"Do you think someone saw it? Or thought they did?"

Raymond's blood felt like frost, and he didn't wait any longer for Josiah's answer. He started running towards town. But then the lantern went out and Josiah came up beside him and threw him to the ground, covering him with his own body and putting his hand over Raymond's mouth.

Chapter 22

* * *

The leather-bound book was a book of the occult. "Intercourse with the Spirits" was its title, though it took a bit of squinting to make it out. The pages had a few handwritten notes in pencil, presumably from the man, but it was at least possible they were from one or more prior owners. Reverend Lowell guessed the book at eighty to one hundred years of age. He would have been interested in it no matter what it contained; he loved old books. But this wasn't mere curiosity. He knew that what Dr. Hall had read had happened not long before this man's arrival and murder. He knew that this book was somehow a part of the murdered man's act. He was concerned about what was next for his town, and for the men who were off in search of the thing, and lastly for Hannibal Guthridge, who could be both a victim and an accomplice of something more sinister than Reverend Lowell would have thought possible in his town yesterday.

He didn't believe in ghosts before this day, and he wouldn't believe in them after. He knew what happened to the dead, and he was confident in God's wisdom in it. What he feared was harder to express in words, even in the words of his thoughts. The warmth, the familiarity of Jason's house didn't help. Everything wicked felt far away here, or at least everything diabolical. But as he read the preface and looked through the first two sections of the volume, he did his best to form his fears in a way he could articulate and then confront. There was something common to both seasons, the one he remembered when the owner of this book had worked considerable mischief before finding himself murdered here in town, and when a violent fire and, he now knew, some grave robbing had occurred, and now, when another murder had occurred, and two new graves were dug up. He felt a chill at the base of his neck and he put his right fingers back there and closed his eyes for a moment. There was an image in his mind that unsettled him, faint as it was. Bright eyes in a shadow larger than it should be. He doubted the image's veracity, as he did with most images, but he still felt that somehow it was close to something true, and it made him wonder whether he was up to this.

What was out there in the world? It was a strange place, he knew, though not as much as the boys he'd grown up with by now would know. He hadn't fought in either of the wars of his generation, and as an adult he'd never been more than a hundred miles away from Sunbury. But he had seen enough to know that God's hand governed no flat and colorless place; there were tall and lively and unpredictable creatures out there in the spaces just past the ends of his hands. There were giants in the days of Noah, and there was a leviathan in the days of Job, and wherever the spark from God's hand had fallen on the earth and kindled life there were

Chapter 22

bound to be beasts and men and angels that he wouldn't understand.

Reverend Lowell never stopped to ask himself whether he truly believed this. He knew what he knew after listening to Josiah Hall, and after seeing that this dead swindler from a lifetime ago had used cheap lies about cheaper magic to inform what he was certain was little more than a stage show. That man fifty years ago had had no intercourse with the dead spirits of men and women. But someone had talked with something that was wicked and deadly. It was not simply a crooked carnival act that had come to town in what seemed to be the first stage of this. And he needed to tell Dr. Hall and Mr. Stanton and Noel Flagler that much.

He thanked Jason, and he embraced him the way he always did, with an understated kiss on the cheek and a pat on the back. Jason was nearly blood, the way Reverend Lowell felt, and while he never showed appreciation for his pastor's fatherliness, he nonetheless felt it. And like all fathers, Reverend Lowell knew. He stepped back out into the evening air and wondered where he might best find Dr. Hall or Mr. Flagler.

* * *

It was standing above them, its breathing strained and fast. It sounded like what Raymond imagined a dying bull would sound like. It smelled like drenched turf.

Raymond considered more in a pair of seconds than he would have thought possible. He wondered when it would kill them, and what being ripped apart would feel like, and whether it would eat them, and why it hadn't struck yet, and whether they could kill it first. He forgot that he was holding his rifle, and for some reason the image of his stabbing it in its eye was in his mind. But then there was a thud as the thing's hands fell to the ground just to the right of Josiah's legs, and its breathing slowed, and then it howled.

Neither of them screamed, each having enough working will to control their sounds, but it was the loudest thing either of them had ever heard. It was far louder than a train whistle. Raymond began to hear a piercing ringing sound that he at first thought was a part of the howl, but then realized his ear had been damaged. It was right as that thought occurred to him that he remembered the rifle, and raised it, squinting as he peered into the darkness for the shape of its head. He couldn't make out anything beyond a vague outline of its bulk, like a huge wave rolling next to them and shading the whispers of moonlight that found their way through the trees. But then he felt Josiah disappear from underneath him, and the thing was running away south, and was far away before he'd fully realized what had happened.

He let air escape his lungs and then stood up. Josiah was gone. The creature was gone. Raymond

Chapter 22

screamed out Josiah's name until his head ached and his throat felt raw, but other than the ringing sound in his ear he heard nothing. He looked back north towards the town and his house, and remembered he couldn't see anything, and turned back in the direction the thing had run, deeper into the woods. He kicked at the ground, hoping Josiah's lantern was down there in the blackness. He even got down on his knees and felt around with his right hand, making sure to keep his rifle in his left so that he didn't lose it, and for what must have been two minutes swept the forest floor everywhere around where they had been hoping to find the lantern. It was not there.

He had kept track of town and which way it had run. He was sure of that, dark or no dark. And so he was certain it had gone south, farther into the forest, and as he stood up he considered what he was to do. After a few seconds, he began walking south, with his right hand outstretched, looking for trees and trying to find his way in the dark.

He was very tired, now well into his second night with almost no sleep, but he didn't have any lack of concentration. The exhaustion only displayed itself in his tripping more times than he would have otherwise, once falling all the way down and scraping his face on the exposed roots of a massive tree that felt harder than stone under his right hand as he pushed himself up.

He had not heard the thing once since it took Josiah, but he knew it was still headed south. All he could do was keep walking as fast as he could in an almost blind night. When the sun began to come up in a few hours, if he hadn't found it yet, he could reconsider his course of action.

He wondered whether Noel Flagler was out here, and he hoped so. Noel would have a far better chance of finding it, and of killing it if he did. They hadn't seen him since late in the afternoon, but he had known Noel's intent was to find whatever had broken his daughter's arm and frightened Hannah Myers and capture or kill it.

It was a mile in front of him by the time he bloodied his cheek on the tree. It had put the man in the cave and was ready to take the life out of him when it closed its eyes instead. It had blood all over its front. Its breathing was fierce and fast and breaking up. Its grip on the man loosened, and it collapsed against the north wall of the cave.

Josiah Hall could barely breathe. He was sure he had at least two broken ribs, and each breath felt like fire. His leg felt broken, too, and he knew there was no way he could sit up. He squinted in the dark, but could see nothing of the creature. He smelled its foul blood and its sweat and skin, and he could hear its breathing slowing, but he couldn't see anything in the darkness of

Chapter 22

the cave. He closed his eyes in the dark and prayed, moving his lips but making no sound.

* * *

Rachel wondered how much longer the night would last. She wished she could kill this thing herself, and the thought made her both angry and afraid, and she found she couldn't hear Mrs. Tufts anymore. Then her legs tightened, and she pushed herself up and began walking to the back of the house, where the tree was. She wouldn't be able to see it without light, so she walked over to Mrs. Tufts and gently touched the back of her hand and then took the lantern from her. Mrs. Tufts was frantic and motherly and crying over Noel, dead on the ground, but she gave up the lantern without much thought, and then knelt down next to Noel and touched his face and cried in a way she had no control over.

Rachel was moving slowly, but with purpose she made her way to the tree. In the dark it looked like a single bony finger stretched up out of the soil. She stepped close enough to touch it, but no closer, and she held the lantern up next to the carving. She looked at the image of her mother carved there by Hell, or by whatever this dark thing was.

Why had it carved her that way? And why had it left that token and not killed Rachel? She wondered how this could be true, how it could be a real occurrence in a real world. She was having trouble hearing anything, now, even Mrs. Tufts' sobbing out in front of the house. The whole moment seemed too immense for her, but she took several deep breaths and found a prayer coming out of her. She discovered there was courage in her to reach her left hand up and touch the rough wood and the carving. She felt two tears slide down her left cheek, and she somehow missed her mother more as she felt the scratch in the bark. It was no more than a mockery, and that's all it was meant to be, and she wondered if the graves it had dug up were the same. Before she could stop herself, she spit onto the carving, though only the biggest of the many droplets landed anywhere near the etchings in the wood. Most went off to the left of the tree, and because of her hatred of the thing and her anger at the fact that she couldn't make it feel the pain of her hate, she screamed, shouting at the tree, and then looked down at the dark ground. In the quiet she heard a howl rise up from out of the woods. An answer to her. She had no fear now. She turned left, towards the woods, and begged that it would come running for her, and that she would get to scratch it with what strength she had left before it crushed her. She set the lantern down on the ground and took ten steps out into the dark, out of its glow, towards the woods far off in the night, and she waited.

Chapter 22

Josiah Hall was right. It wanted her. Whatever it was, it wanted her. She would use that to fight it for whatever few seconds she could, because it had thought it could touch something precious with its vile fingers.

* * *

Reverend Lowell found he couldn't sleep. He had given no thought to his sermon for the coming Lord's Day all day, which was unusual for him. He wanted to speak to Noel Flagler, or to Dr. Hall, and the fact that he hadn't was troubling him, as though he couldn't conceive of the answer to an easy arithmetic problem. Or as though there were a riddle he had known the answer to as a child, but that was now escaping him despite all his best attempts to recall it.

He had never felt his heart palpitate before, and its doing so now as he lay under his wool blanket and stared up into the darkness of his bedroom made him even more tense. The image of the fire, though he hadn't seen it as a young man, was in his mind, and he had only the barest idea of why. If the murderer of the spiritualist who'd stayed during that time at the Inn was responsible for the fire, he couldn't imagine such a man also being responsible for what had happened in the cemetery. Fifty years had passed, and his own back pain was evidence of what five successive decades do to a man.

If it weren't a man? He knew that is what Dr. Hall thought. And he supposed that was why he wanted to speak with him as much as he did Noel. Dr. Hall had a conception of what sort of a menace they were protecting against, and if he were right, then *only* he was right. Reverend Lowell wasn't convinced of it, and he doubted Noel Flagler would hear of anything so fantastic. A man or men had dug up the graves, and Hannibal Guthridge had murdered Ed Aimes, and a man or an animal had frightened the Stanton girl and her neighbors and injured her.

As he surrendered to his sleeplessness, he decided that he could walk while praying, and so rose up from the bed and put both hands on his bureau. The ache in his back spread upwards towards his shoulders and he winced for a moment as it pulsed with his palpitations. After it subsided to a duller ache, he got dressed and put on his coat, knowing that despite the warmth outside his bones would still be cold.

He heard crickets and the rustling of the tall grass as he stepped out his front door, and though the wind felt chill to him he knew it was warm to everyone else, and pleasant, so he stopped just outside his door and breathed deeply, trying to enjoy what he could of the moment. He was an old man, there was no debating that. He was near enough to the grave to have settled the thought of death in his mind. But he still did very much like this earth and this town and the people he

Chapter 22

lived here with, and so smiled despite his fear of what was out there or who might be troubling Sunbury, and despite his anxiety over the soul and life of the ornery and wicked Hannibal Guthridge.

He began walking, unsure of where he was going. He had prayed through the second and the fourth Psalms in his mind when he heard a woman's shout in the distance, and his heart stung and beat oddly in his chest before his mind had even registered it. The image of the fire was in his head again, and then of Hannibal's face and of Ed Aimes' funeral service, which hadn't even happened yet. He looked in the direction of the shout and squinted into the dark, but he could see nothing other than a dozen or so lamps glowing in windows in that direction, southwest towards the Mason Street and the jagged Limestone Street and the outer rim of town.

He found his legs frozen to the spot, and that troubled him nearly as much as the sound. He couldn't remember ever being immobile from fear that way, not even twelve years ago when a drunken man had stumbled into a Lord's Day service while he was still preaching. He had spoken loudly to the man warning that he was in danger of angering the Almighty and that he'd best sit down and let his blood cool and his eyes close and listen to the Word, and that afterward he could speak to him. The man had, and when he'd started to snore, Ed Aimes had gone to him and quietly told him to stop it. Reverend Lowell had always been able to soldier on through fear. But now he was stuck to the dry dirt of the lane he'd been walking on, and he didn't seem to have control of any of his limbs.

* * *

Raymond's face stung and ached. He gave it almost no thought, though, as he marched through the night as quickly as he could, his left hand stretched out in front of him to feel for the trees he couldn't see. He was scared that Josiah would be dead already, and he was scared that he would miss their only chance to kill whatever it was before it went for his daughter again.

Rose.

What he missed about his wife at night was the feel of her form in the bed. She was present, there as a woman, a reality to be reckoned with in all her obstinate, glorious, subtle personality. Memories could be held on to, turned over in his mind as he applied grease to the hinge for his daughter's chicken coop door or turned the wheel at the well in early morning. The thoughts of past moments were free to him as long as his mind had them to recall. But the real woman, her red-brown hair and how she might choose to put it up on any one given day, the way she startled him sometimes with a sudden, sharp burst of laughter like a drop of ice-cold water down the back of his shirt, the

Chapter 22

distinct, salty, otherness of who she really was and the unchangeable nature of her covenanted marriage to him, that was all irrevocably taken away. So, at least fifty times since she'd died, Raymond had either had trouble falling asleep or woken up in the night to expect her there and then been unable to return to sleep. His love wasn't blind to Rose's real faults; he hadn't constructed a false Rose in his mind from carefully selected memories. But love is as at least as real as its object, and he loved Rose Stanton from this side of the grave with all he had.

There was a stray dog he'd seen walking through the avenue in front of their house once a week or so after they'd moved to Sunbury, and he'd whistled and motioned with his hand for the dog to come to him, waving confidently but with tempered excitement toward himself, like a man who was happy but tired. The dog had looked at him but kept walking north down the avenue, but after about five steps it came and squatted and he patted its head, bright brown like fresh wet dirt just exposed from under live turf. There was white in it, too, and the white was brighter than he might have expected on a dog with no owner. He looked in its eyes, and they were bright, and it had tilted its head to its right when he'd finished petting and scratching it, and when he stood, he'd felt a tightness in his chest and in his back that he'd never felt before. There was something in him that awakened at the gentle, unassuming presence of a dog, a dog that had no questions for him about why he had moved to Sunbury or where he was from or whether he would remarry or how he would care for his remaining child. He felt exposed to something alive for the first time since the second Lord's Supper he'd taken after Rose's death, when the wine and the bread had stung his soul and his tongue like hot lightning and he'd not been able to stop himself from crying. But he'd made no sounds and kept his breathing normal, and no one had seen except Lorinda McClellan, who said nothing because she knew the kind of man Raymond was and the kind of sorrow he was walking with.

He'd stood then, with the same heat and the same tightness, and he'd smiled at the dog, and then he'd knelt down again to pet it, but it ran off southward, in the opposite direction from which it had come, and Raymond never saw it again, and never thought about it again until now.

He heard something in the distance that sounded like crunching, and he stopped and held up the rifle in his right hand. His chest tightened and he thought of Rachel, and he slowed his breathing as best he could. The cracking, crunching sound continued for another few seconds, and he thought that it moved just a little to the west. And that if it wasn't wind in the treetops, it was something very large on the ground a few hundred yards in front of him. He decided it wasn't the wind

Chapter 22

since there wasn't any creaking of branches, and since it seemed to be localized to one place, and he waited.

* * *

It had come for her. The man with the book had been a call to it, but she was what it wanted to crush. Long after the man with the book, the whispers of the liar it loved had told it of a new hunt, the one for her, had told it how the mother and the brother had been slain. But she was the flame that must be put out. And it had savored the hunt.

It put its hand on its chest and closed its eyes and called upon the skin to re-stitch under the dark blood and waited. The man was next to it in the dark, barely breathing. It would break his neck when the skin was restored.

"You won't get her."

It knew the words, but it wanted silence. It would have ripped his tongue out if it could have moved.

We will burn them all, it spoke in answer.

"I beg to differ," the man spoke into darkness not even its eyes could see through. It heard a sound on the man's form, a sound it didn't recognize. It knew now the man could be doing something to harm it.

"The smallest thought Jehovah has is wider than the sky, and here you are, barely taller than my grandmother's rose bush, thinking you can stand against Him. I'd reconsider whose soil you're leaning on."

It bit its tongue at the mention of the name. It hated the language the man was speaking, and it hated the name.

It could not make, but it could destroy. And the pain on its chest would kill it or would move to another part of its body now that it was closing the wound. But it would destroy the man, all of them, and then the girl. It would leave her in the dirt of the place as it burned.

Josiah Hall had pulled the vial of white arsenic he'd taken from his office out of his pocket and was holding it now. It wasn't broken, which he had trusted God for. Now he trusted that he could pull himself a foot or two closer to it without it realizing. And so he did. His trousers scraped the floor of the cave, but it did not move. It had to have heard him in the quiet, but he did not hear it move, and it didn't speak again. He was terrified, but he was resolved. He thought of Rachel Stanton's face as it looked in her house a few hours before, right next to Mrs. Tufts' shoulder, and he had no remorse about this being the end of his life on earth. He flipped the cork out of the vial with his left thumb, and when he smelled the wet, dirty smell of its skin and blood and felt the heat coming off its body, he gave himself a second to discern where its chest was in the dark. It was between seven and eight feet tall, and its upper body was resting on the north wall of the cave

Chapter 22

just in front of him. From where he was, down on his belly, he would have to reach up two or more feet to stick the vial into the wound. He would have to raise himself up. He found an outcrop of limestone jutting out from the wall a few inches, and without any more thought he pushed himself with his right hand and brought his left hand down just to the right of the wound in its broad, strong chest. He was able to find the blood and the open spot before it came down on him like lightning, and then Josiah saw darkness before he saw light.

* * *

Rachel and Mrs. Tufts had called Joel Fremont, knowing that Noel Flagler was dead, and that Dr. Hall was out in the woods now with Rachel's father. He had help from two other men in getting Noel to his parlor, and once they were gone Rachel felt emptier and confused. She knew someone had to go tell Mrs. Flagler, and the thought of Patricia Flagler sobbing and the two boys wondering what was wrong made her sick. The pain in her arm began to throb again, and she was sure she would retch right there outside her front door.

Somehow the moment passed, though, and Mrs. Tufts came up and embraced her, and kissed the back of her head, and Rachel, though irritated at the contact and the scent of perfume when her stomach felt so turbulent, took the gesture as it was intended and returned the embrace. Then the two of them stepped into the house to collect themselves before walking to the Flaglers' home. Two steps in, Mrs. Tufts screamed so loudly that Rachel was sure the thing was inside their house again. She jumped and Mrs. Tufts' arm fell from Rachel's shoulders, and she saw out of the corner of her eyes that she had put both hands to her mouth. There was a moment of slowness as Rachel tried not to look where she was looking, down at the floor near where Rachel had been sitting when the thing had come in. Rachel knew that it was whatever it had thrown at her feet that was scaring Mrs. Tufts. She looked down without wanting to, and saw a severed arm on the floor, dirty and caked in dried blood and with the remains of a white shirt still clinging to it up to the shoulder. She felt the room begin to swim around her, but she knew she had to stay conscious, that she must not faint and land on her broken arm, so she breathed deep breaths, and made herself think of the back of their property in sunlight, and with summer wind rustling the leaves on the trees and the tall grass and tried to remember what clean daylight smelled like.

* * *

Reverend Lowell had found the will and energy to move, but it seemed to him that he was above himself

Chapter 22

somewhere in the air, and that whatever man was moving now was a different one. He couldn't feel the breeze, or the chill that only he felt, or even the dull ache in his back. There were enough lanterns in windows to guide his steps through the dark to the source of the scream. No one else had come yet, but it was Raymond Stanton's house, and the door was open, and he could see the single flickering light of a lantern down on the ground or on a low table or in someone's hand just inside the door. He still didn't feel much as he walked to the door and said, "Is anyone in need of assistance?" but he seemed to regain his senses when he saw Mrs. Abigail Tufts' pale face in the scattered glow of the yellow light coming from the lantern in her hand. She was horrified by something, and Raymond Stanton's daughter was leaning forward next to her, looking at the bloody mess of an arm on the floor. Without any way of knowing how he knew, Reverend Lowell knew it was Hannibal Guthridge's arm, and he walked over to the women and put a hand on either of their shoulders.

"Are you all right, ladies? What has happened?"

"Noel Flagler is dead," Mrs. Tufts answered. "He was killed out front not an hour ago after firing at the thing that came in this house. And it left that!" She closed her eyes, and then pulled in Rachel, forgetting about the girl's broken arm, and scolding herself silently when Rachel Stanton cried out.

Nephilim

Reverend Lowell gave her a moment to speak again, knowing Mrs. Tufts well enough to know that she was likely not done talking, but she had her eyes closed and her lower lip under her upper teeth and her cheek buried in Rachel Stanton's hair. Reverend Lowell gave them both an embrace, then took the lantern from Abigail Tufts' hand and stepped up to the arm on the Stanton's front room floor. He had to force himself to crouch down next to it and lower the lantern down near it where he could see it more clearly. All the way up to the white flesh of the fingers it was covered in darkening blood, dried blood that looked almost black except where the flickering light landed on it. The fingers were whiter than a living man's arm where they weren't caked in the dried blood. Without allowing himself to think much about it, he used the remains of the shirt to pick up the arm and carry it outside, where the women wouldn't have to see it anymore. He set it in the grass a few feet from Raymond Stanton's front door, and then looked left and right through the darkness, towards town and then towards the woods. No one else had come, and he couldn't see any movement anywhere. He wondered if it were truly gone, and what it was, and how he could keep the women safe with no rifle or weapon. Then he thought of Noel Flagler's wife and his children, and wondered who would tell them and who would see to Hannibal.

Chapter 22

He decided he would and went in and told Rachel and Abigail.

* * *

It would start the fire. Whether death would find it was a thought with no weight to it. It could feel the tightness and the stinging spreading inside now, no doubt from whatever the man had put inside its wound, but it would dispense death, and if death fell to it as well, the transaction would be worth it. The man and his book had been a sound like the whispers, and it had come for them because it had sensed blood. There were men and women worth breaking where it had heard him.

It had taken the bones and the flesh of men and women and children from the earth because of the whispers, and because of its hunger to make death as ugly as it could. Death was its weapon against God, against the name, against the maker and his law and his tyranny and his sameness. It gloried in death because it hated him.

It had arms and legs and a mouth and speech like they did, but it wasn't one of them. They were the chosen sons and daughters, and so it enjoyed inflicting pain and death and violence on them. It had obeyed the whispers for most of its life, and so it was here in this place, in the trees and the caves and the shadows outside their houses and streets, and it sought her.

Reverend Lowell burned Marvin Branson's book the night the monster came into town to destroy Sunbury.

* * *

Rachel didn't want to have to say that she would go with him, but she wanted to go. The saying was hard, her world felt heavy, and the words seemed to have a cost to them she didn't want to indulge, and the last thing she wanted to do was talk to Reverend Lowell or persuade him that she was serious. But she did say it, and her eyes closed after she did, and her broken arm felt like it was burning on the inside. But Reverend Lowell surprised her by not saying anything, and when she opened her eyes, he smiled at her in the dark of the room, and she felt warm tears coming down her face. She loved him then, and she loved Mrs. Tufts, and she was terrified of being killed by the thing, and she was furious that it had taken the father of two little boys and the husband of a Christian woman of her church, and she was never more sure of anything than that she had said the right thing.

The two of them walked out into the night, and Abigail Tufts walked silently just a pace behind them. She would go home, she'd said, and she seemed to be

Chapter 22

struck dumb for the moment, at least until they were out into the street and away from the Stanton's house and Hannibal's arm and the place where Noel had been laying in the grass. Then she came up next to Rachel and whispered something in her ear. There was a bright lamp in the window of a house on Beadle Street as they crossed it and made their way for the Tufts' house, and inside the window was a man Reverend Lowell didn't know. His face was dark, and he had pronounced lines on his forehead and was simply staring out at the night as they walked by. The reverend considered that there might be less than twenty people in Sunbury whose names or faces he didn't know, and he'd just happened upon one of them. It made him wonder, not for the first time, what sort of a pastor would take over once he was gone. He was anxious at the thought of someone he didn't know preaching to the people, and offering them counsel and guidance, baptizing their children and giving the eulogies at their funerals. He remembered the first funeral he ever performed in Sunbury was on a Thursday, and it rained, and no one spoke a word during the entire service. He remembered all those things not so much because it was his first funeral as because it was a child, a little yellow-haired boy called Charlie, and he had had no idea until then just how much of a hollow death left behind it. The boy's mother, whose name he couldn't recall for some reason, which troubled him now so much that he bit the inside of his cheek as they walked in silence, had sobbed openly and violently, but she formed no words, and he was in awe of the power of the woman's feeling. She was hot with sadness and anger. He remembered struggling with what to say to her or to the boy's father, not having been married or having children himself. He felt the weight of their sadness, everyone who looked at them did, but he could think of nothing to say to them that would have the thickness of reality to it coming from his own bachelor lips. And so he'd prayed silently even as he read Scripture, and he asked that God would bless the poor woman with hope and faith, and when he'd finally spoken to them he'd barely gotten any words out before he began to cry himself, though having never known the boy alive. And the father had then shaken his hand, and the mother embraced him, and he'd thought then that he would die for such people if it came to it, and the thought had somehow comforted him then that he had chosen the right profession.

He stopped biting his cheek and stopped walking. He hadn't chosen anything. This town and this calling had chosen him. Abigail and Rachel were still walking. They apparently hadn't yet noticed that he had stopped. They had no shadows now in the street since there were no lights in any of the windows around them. He knew he couldn't lose sight of them, he couldn't leave them alone tonight, and yet he was drowning in the thought,

Chapter 22

for the first time he could remember, that he had not contrived his own existence. He had not made himself pastor of his church, or son of his father Lewis Lowell, or even unmarried all these years. It seemed to him now that he had been a witness to his life. But he knew that wasn't right. He was responsible for his sins and for his faults, not a mere observer of them. But as he considered the boy's father and mother at that funeral, thought about the tears that had overwhelmed him as much as any sickness he'd ever had, something he could neither explain nor resolve, he accepted that in some real way he was at the mercy of another in everything he had ever done and ever undertaken.

* * *

Raymond heard the crunching for another second, then the treetops were rustling in the dark. It sounded like a wind that was sudden and furious, and then he heard the creaking of branches that told him something was moving along the trees, further down. As the sound came closer he instinctively raised the rifle and felt the blood rush to his ears and eyes and chills run up his neck. He gritted his teeth as the sound came over his head, and he realized it was climbing down the tree above him much faster than any man could move. He stepped back six steps without lowering his rifle just as it thudded to the soil a foot from where he'd been standing. Without thinking he fired the rifle and screamed in anger. He was holding it perfectly and didn't move at all from the discharge; the shout of fury at the thing was all the flourish his instincts allowed him. Everything else was as it should be if you wanted to put a shot in something to kill it. In the single flash of light from the rifle's barrel he'd seen nothing, but he fancied that he had seen it in a moment that felt drawn out, when he seemed to have a hundred thoughts at once, waiting to hear it die or feel it toss him up into the air and tear him apart. He saw in his mind a black mound of hair with red eyes and the teeth of a bear and a mouth that was warm and fierce and almost glowed. He felt Rachel's smooth cheek against his, and he did what he needed to do to fire again. He shouted during that shot as well, then he stepped forward in an anger he'd never felt before, anger that seemed to go down to the bedrock of the earth a mile beneath his feet, anger that carried him closer to the creature in an orbit he was no more free to disobey than the moon could its own. He let the rifle fall from his hands and pulled a knife from a sheath at his side and gripped it hard in his right hand and then pulled his right arm up to his face so that the blade was in front of him and just to the left of his head. He heard the thing howl as loud as any noise he'd ever heard, but he didn't flinch. He'd expected that.

He felt the grass under his boots and the warm air on his skin and noticed the tightness in all his muscles

Chapter 22

as he waited to feel the thing on him, clawing or pulling him apart or fighting him with whatever life and strength it had left. He knew it was possible his shots hadn't landed at all, but he intended to cut it to pieces either way, or to die in the attempt, and moved forward with no hesitancy. At the third step it howled again and he felt himself lose hearing altogether now, a ringing in his head making him squint and the left ear hurting enough to register in his mind despite his focus on killing it. Then it kicked him, as he saw just enough to know that it was now on the ground just in front of him. He fell back, too quickly to keep his head from hitting the ground directly, and he thought he would faint as he lost his grip on the knife. But he didn't faint, and as it grabbed his shirt he reached out with his fingers and found the handle right there on his chest and began to swing the blade furiously as it pulled him toward itself. The first swing had some resistance, so he knew he'd cut it, but the fourth felt as though he'd tried to slice the trunk of an old tree, and it howled again. He smiled when it did, then he felt himself drop a foot or so into the darkness. He smelled its musk, old and damp, and it knocked his face to the ground as it thrashed in injury. He reached out with his right hand, the knife gone now, hoping for something else he could do to it, then his head felt strangely warm and everything was black.

23
1843

Theodore found the stream in the daylight. It seemed cold despite the sun's early morning brightness. The water looked to be only a few feet deep at most. It wasn't quite clear, but even from where he was, twenty or so paces away from its eastern bank, he thought he could make out the bottom. Both banks were rocky, and on the other side a steep limestone ridge rose up ten or twelve feet. The sun was bright on that cliff wall and he saw now that there were scratches in it, more than a dozen of them, and he began to be afraid. Instinctively he stepped further out into the sunlight, and the direct light and warmth on the back of his neck reminded him of how much he hurt. He was afraid of touching his neck in the place the pain was coming from. He remembered the stiff, blinding pain last night, and he knew he needed a doctor, and was worried that he had some irreversible damage to his neck or spine.

He heard the crunch of the pebbles as he got closer to the stream, and he began to realize that though he welcomed the sunlight, he was also completely visible now. There were no places to hide from it. He stopped moving about five paces from the bank of the stream and tried to focus on the moving water, rippling over stones in a southerly direction, deeper and deeper into the forest. The sound of the

Chapter 23

water was good, and he closed his eyes and let it calm him as much as it could. Then he heard the crunching of steps over the pebbles again, behind him. He found he couldn't move. He couldn't even tap his foot. The fear he had was unlike any he'd ever felt, even the first time when this creature had almost killed him. He tried to open his eyes and was surprised to see that he could do that. There was a shadow to his left, stretching out over the ground, out over the stream, and up onto the cliff wall on the other side. He lost control of most of his body as he looked at the shadow's shape. It was like a man's, but the shoulders, or what he assumed were shoulders, were much bigger, and more rounded. The head was squatter. The arms were out to either side and he thought that they seemed to be a bit shorter in relation to its trunk than a man's would be, but much more muscular. He heard something very much like a snort. The sound was more breath than moisture. It sounded much like a bull's snort.

Strangely, Theodore thought about when he'd murdered Marvin. His partner had done nothing to him. He remembered what it had felt like to kill Marvin, something he'd indeed thought about doing no less than ten times before he did it, and the same sense of delight crept through him now, scared as he was, as did then. He'd hated Marvin. It was as simple as that. He hated his demeanor, his showmanship, his pretension of intelligence. He'd wanted to murder someone for years. He felt no regret for it, even though he began to think he would be dead himself in a few seconds, and he wasn't at all sure what would happen to him after that. But he certainly believed Marvin Branson was owed no more consideration than he'd given to him, and so the thoughts of the crime settled somewhere in his mind as he decided he might try to turn around and look at the creature before it devoured him. The thought of Christ's parable of the rich man and Lazarus flashed through his mind, though he had no idea why, and hated it.

He hadn't seen the thing clearly, certainly not in daylight. He expected to be mesmerized. But when he turned to take his best look, it leaped over him, over the stream, and to the top of the cliff on the other bank. Then it was gone, running west somewhere on the other side of the cliff. He had felt the wind coming off it as it jumped over him, smelled the ancient, earthy smell it carried with it, and seen that it was blacker than night against the blue sky above him before it had disappeared down what must be a gradual decline on the other side of the limestone wall.

Theodore stood stunned. He hadn't seen it in the daylight, and it hadn't destroyed him. He felt his blood begin to run through his body fast and warm again, and he smiled. He took his glasses off and polished them with his shirt, as he often did when in deep thought. This was a beast of human intelligence, and it had seen

Chapter 23

something in him that had made it spare his life. Theodore was still afraid of death, but his curiosity and excitement were too much for him as they called him deeper into the woods. He leaped over the stream at the narrowest point he could find, then walked into the trees on the other side.

24

1892

Reverend Lowell turned back to the women and then heard the call from away up right, out in the dark off the beaten dirt of the street. It sounded incomplete and strained, like a drunk man shouting an unfamiliar name, but after a moment he realized it had been the word "Woman!"

He looked in that direction and began to wonder if there was a brawl going on somewhere out in the shadows, but then he heard the report of a rifle shot, and saw Abigail Tufts jump and scream, and he collected enough of himself to run up to her and Rachel and step in front of them. As he did, he heard a slow laugh, maniacal and wistful and unreasonable, sounding like the laugh of a man whose mind was thoroughly undone, and he saw Hannibal Guthridge step into the dim light of the street towards them.

"I know," he said. Reverend Lowell shook the impression that he was dreaming from his mind. Hannibal wasn't dead, but he was out of the custody of the room where he'd been stored by Noel, and he was clearly mad.

"It killed those boys that came back to bring me supper," he said, and he smiled in a way that made the Reverend wonder if he had ever seen the world as properly as he was called to. He had no category for the

Chapter 24

sickness of Hannibal's smile, lifted up on only one side of his old and angry face, revealing a few teeth on the right side of his jaw and bringing no change to his eyes. Hannibal was ugly in every way a man can be ugly, and he was intent on killing one or both women, and in the span of several seconds Reverend Lowell decided he would have to kill him first and not regret it.

"You don't know what it is," Hannibal said, his voice rising towards the end of the sentence so that he was almost shouting. "I know, but you don't! And I know what you are, too! I know now and I've always known!" Reverend Lowell decided Hannibal was talking to the Stanton girl, and he knew he'd have to wait until he took a few more steps towards them before he could make a move. Hannibal didn't seem ready to shoot just yet, and it would be better to wait until his old frame could grab him in one step than to try to preempt him and fail and leave the women to be shot in the street.

Hannibal took a small step towards the three of them, further into the dim light of a lantern in a house ten paces or so behind them. His arm was bloody but intact. It hadn't been his on the Stanton's floor. He raised the rifle a bit more so that it was pointed at their heads, now, and he laughed. Reverend Lowell decided there was no more time.

* * *

Nephilim

The sound of wind in the treetops woke it up. There was fire in its chest, the sensation of a stinging pressure, and it was struggling to take breaths. It held the beginnings of a thought for a few seconds: Disbelief that after thousands of summers in the long shadows of trees like these it would now face death. The man with the red hair had put something inside it, and the wounds it had received from the two others were hot with pain.

It wanted to see her before it died. It wanted to show her what it was and what it could break. Then it would take the breath from out of her body and revel in what it had undone.

And there was the other man. The old one. He had heard the whispers, too. Not in the same way it did, but with the same words. That creature could finish what it started.

A sound came in the wind, then, and the thought was gone. Something was happening in the town. It pressed its feet down into the soil and stood despite the pain. Then it picked up the father and began walking.

It remembered. It considered the blood that it put down in the soil. The world had as much blood as it could take, but it was never enough. The lust it felt for mocking what God was fond of was a hole inside it that had no bottom. There couldn't be enough bodies of men and women and children to rip up out of the dirt and show to his face and to the faces of all his angels.

Chapter 24

And hers was the face that had the most fire, a fire that must be put out.

It didn't need the whispers to know that she was a spark of great brightness. It saw the shine just as clearly as Hell did. He had made her and marked her for something, and it would savor squeezing all of that call out of her lungs along with her last breaths and her last pleadings with the God it hated. It would savor putting her up on the highest hill out in the woods, where tomorrow's sun would light up her breathless and broken body. Then it could die, but not before.

She would die first.

It grunted its pleasure from deep in its old chest, then fell to its knees and dropped Raymond Stanton, not intending to. It closed its eyes and struggled to stand again.

Josiah Hall's poison stretched through every part of its body, and it fell down on all fours, clawing at the dirt with its hands in a confusion that was as new to it as electricity. It stretched its body in an effort to relieve the forceful ache it felt in its abdomen and the lower part of its chest. The pain was suddenly the worst it had yet known. Its eyes were closed as Raymond came to and pulled out the knife. And when it howled again, Raymond didn't flinch. He plunged the knife into its outstretched neck. Then the howling stopped, and his dark world was spinning as he felt himself flying through the air.

Nephilim

* * *

Reverend Lowell wondered for two or three seconds whether he would actually be able to kill a man. He'd never even hit a man in anger before. But then something older and wilder took over his arms and legs and the rest of him, and when Hannibal was within a stone's throw of them, he moved like lightning to grab Hannibal's rifle. Reverend Lowell heard the shot, and he smelled it like bad firewood as he grabbed the barrel and pulled it down towards the ground. Hannibal let go and screamed louder than Reverend Lowell would have thought possible, and his eyes seemed to be almost yellow, like a tomcat's in low light. Then Reverend Lowell found his hand around Hannibal's throat, and he was squeezing much too tightly for Hannibal to do any more screaming, and he was pulling the old man's tight, wiry body down to the dirt of the street.

There was blood down there, like thin red paint in the dry dirt of the street. It all seemed to be happening so fast, and Reverend Lowell's confused mind thought that it was Hannibal's blood somehow. The thought didn't make him loosen his grip on the old man's neck, though. There was a viciousness in Hannibal's face, his eyes squinting and yet seeming to widen in their focused intent on killing them all and in his lips pulled back to bare his old teeth. Reverend Lowell knew he could never let go. Not until Hannibal

Chapter 24

was dead. But his hands started loosening anyway, and he felt Hannibal pull himself from his grip, and saw him pull back and away from him quickly like a wild dog, though it was harder to see him now because everything was blurry. He reached out his right hand to grab Hannibal's ankle before he could stand up, but the hand wouldn't go much further than a few inches from his own body. Then he felt a stabbing pain in the top of his head, and then he saw nothing more.

* * *

Rachel thought she screamed. She was sure she screamed. But then she felt her lips still unparted, hot and tingling like the rest of her face, and she knew that it had been Mrs. Tufts. She couldn't turn to look at her, though. Hannibal Guthridge held her gaze as certainly as if she were a puppet he was toying with. She watched his hunched form step back into the slightly brighter light in the street, reach down to Reverend Lowell while still staring into her, and pick his rifle back up. Reverend Lowell tried to grab the gun from Hannibal, but the old man brought its handle down hard on the Reverend's head, sounding like an axe on a tree trunk, and as Rachel winced and worried about her pastor's head his body went completely still.

"You don't know anything," Hannibal whispered at her, and she had a moment's thought as he did that she might be able to run quickly across the street and grab the gun while he was focused on talking. But then she knew she couldn't do it. She would fall, or he would simply have enough time to raise and fire, and she would be dead, and then Mrs. Tufts would be, too. She wondered if Reverend Lowell were already dead, and she prayed silently, not even moving her lips, asking God that it not be so and that she and Mrs. Tufts not die and that her father and Dr. Hall be home before the sun came up. She found she was not so afraid of dying as of not doing what was right, and somehow that thought slowed things down for her. She reached her hand back to find Mrs. Tufts', and when she found only air she began to turn, but then she heard Hannibal scream. She looked back just in time to see him crumple to the ground, his body blanketed in shadow not far from Reverend Lowell's.

* * *

All it felt was pain now. Hot, blinding pain in its throat, and the pressure in its chest and gut from what the other man had put in it. Everything took effort, even stumbling, crawling on the ground, and the air and the terrain and the tree trunks seemed confusing and unfamiliar to its senses. Was it going up a hill? Or on level ground and simply having that much trouble moving? It hadn't been confused in this way since the

Chapter 24

first time this had happened, the night with the murderer, the night it had intended to burn it all. It felt it needed more air than it could get into its lungs with the short breaths it could take, each feeling like fire and getting caught on the blood and gore in its throat. The pain made its hate clearer. It wanted everything dead. It wanted to scar God's world deep enough that God might feel it and mourn it. It gritted its teeth and hoped the old man would get the girl. And then suddenly it felt the ground turn to air underneath its right hand, and it was falling through a blurred darkness, and it managed a final word from its harsh heart before its head hit rock. It died at the bottom of a dry creek bed, one that would be flooded with the next good rain.

25

1843

Theodore would have given nearly anything to find it again. Not his life, certainly, but nearly anything. He had to see it again in the daylight. He had to know if it was like a man, if it could think and talk and reason. He had to know why it hadn't attacked him, and why it had appeared like such a violent force on the roof during Branson's presentation. He knew it was malevolent, and he suspected it was demonic, arriving when it did and where it did. But he wasn't sure, and even if he were, he still had to know what it was and where it had come from and what it did.

His feet crunched the warm, dry summer ground just on the other side of the wall he'd now left behind. He could hear the sound of a few birds somewhere in the distance, and the thick, gentle sound of leaves rustling lightly above his head like sheets of wet newspaper, and a dragonfly or a bumblebee somewhere not far from his head. But he did not hear the movement in the distance he'd hoped to hear, far enough away that he might have been able to trail it and merely catch a clear glimpse of it from some far elevated point, then slowly trudge back to the village. There was no sound of ground under foot far off ahead, no sound of branches breaking, no sound of breathing or any other noise he could attribute to it. He

Chapter 25

felt his chest tightening and the hair on the back of his neck lifting up. Theodore trusted his body, as a rule. It would usually tell him the truth about threats. He knew that there was nothing else he had been thinking of that could make him afraid out in these woods. He wondered what it was that he had seen or heard but as of yet not been conscious of, what could make his skin and organs react the way they were now. He stood stock still and looked from left to right at the shadows, long and gray in the summer sun under the trees and swept them with all his powers of sight for anything that could mean it was here but silent.

To his left was a gully, a drop in the ground towards what might be another creek. It was a hundred yards or so away, and though he felt naked in this particular part of the forest since the trees, younger and thinner, were much further apart than what he'd been looking through since entering the woods, he began to walk towards it, gingerly and with care not to step on anything that would make a loud noise.

He was curious. He was always curious. The world intrigued him, though without fail he always held it in contempt after he discovered what was on the other side of the door. Even killing Marvin hadn't been as satisfying as he'd hoped, and he'd known it before Marvin had hit the ground. But the feverish need to know what the creature was racked him with an intensity he hadn't known before. He was willing to be hurt or nearly killed again to find out. He didn't suppose this was true, but it was at least conceivable that he was willing to die and face whatever Hell he knew he had coming in finding out. And the feeling of heat and compulsion only grew as he stepped through the thin shadows of this newer patch of trees and to the small scar in the earth where he now saw exposed rock.

It was, indeed, a steep drop. He could get down with care on the bit of exposed rock and crumbled topsoil to his left, especially as the roots of a maple tree stretched out into the air and then wound down towards the floor below like old, hungry fingers. He saw on the floor of the small ravine a layer of new soil that had crumbled from the edges. It seemed to him as though a mountain giant had reached down with his fist and drug it along the forest floor for a piece, leaving a wound in the earth for the woods to reclaim someday, if they could.

He tumbled down into the ravine like a drunk falling down a flight of stairs. Theodore generally had good control of his body and good sense, but the problem was that he hadn't known how soft the rock and dirt that formed the walls of the little ravine were. His right heel slipped just as he was tightening his grip on the roots of a tree, and he landed on the ground on the bottom on his back and with the pain in his head sharp again and almost making him cry out. He stopped himself just before the first sound left his throat, and he

Chapter 25

was grateful for that. But he was even more certain now that this was not a natural ravine whose age was coincident with the forest's. Something new and recent had formed this gash in the ground that was perhaps twelve feet deep and twenty-five-feet wide, uneven and crooked as it stretched out and away to the south, then bending to the east so that he couldn't see how far it went. He felt cold as he tried to quietly stand, and he gripped the back of his head as he tried to will the pain down and away and consider whether he was standing in something associated with the creature. He wondered whether it could bend the earth to its will, if it was indeed some sort of supernatural being. But while it was an intriguing idea, he dismissed it after a moment's thought as either unlikely or simply too fanciful to have anything he could do with without further evidence. Theodore's fascination with the world was practical in that regard. He held interest in the phenomena of God's world, but the mere consideration of the world and its curiosities didn't arouse much in him. He had to actually hold the pieces of the puzzle and then put them together if he were to have any excitement.

He shook his head, regretting it immediately as the pain spun behind his eyes like an angry fire, and then began to walk further into the ravine. The ground was so much scattered soil, clumpy and claylike under some of his stops, powdery and dry in others. But the floor of the cut through the earth was not so uneven and cluttered that it was as though he were walking down the remnants of the landslide. One good rainstorm would wash much of this dirt away, and then there would be a flat new creek bed here. What was he walking in?

As he got to where he hadn't been able to see any further from the beginning of the ravine, or what he thought of as its beginning, he looked across it and saw that as it stretched south, to his left, there was a ribcage hanging from an exposed log jutting out of the ground that made up the wall on the opposite side. A man's ribcage, the first, second, and fifth ribs on the right side broken away, peering down at him from ten feet up in the air and thirty feet away. He felt his heartbeat in his palms, and there was a buzzing in his ears that made it hard to move and to think. *This was a mistake. I should never have come here.* He knew it was true, and yet he also knew he would keep descending. He was certain the creature had killed the man, and he knew it was doing something evil beyond any thought of his own in hanging some of his remains as though they were a banner proclaiming its intent. And Theodore was aware of the fact that it meant something strange that there was no flesh on the bones. They were dirty white, the color of a very old man's eyes, flecked with dirt but standing out like a half-moon against the dark brown of the soil of the ravine's opposite wall. Theodore wondered what man they had been in, what type of skin

Chapter 25

had once encased them, and his natural curiosity, animal and lively as ever, redirected some of his energy away from his panic and made the thrumming in his ears stop. He wondered if he were a farmer from the village, who might have been taking in air on a morning of sunshine and light wind just under those ribs on the day the creature killed him. He smiled a little, something he always did when he considered the power involved in inflicting pain, fear, death. He was attracted to that power the way most children were attracted to the smell of baking pies. It gave him delight and warmth and excitement and hope down in the deepest parts of his soul. He closed his eyes for a moment and pictured the now dead man's hair rustling in the light breeze, and the huge black creature just beginning to rise up over a hill at the edge of the man's property, just a few yards behind him, while the man leaned on his wooden fence and considered his property and had no idea that the thing, silent, was stalking him.

He was ushered back into his present reality by the sound of scraping and clawing and huffing, and his body felt charged and cold at the same time. He spent two seconds determining that the sound was in front of him, further into the ravine as it bent away south, and after deciding that he had to know what the creature was doing, should the sound be it, he took four of the softest and most silent steps of his life. From the perch of that fourth step, after he raised himself up on his toes at the top of a slight hill of new soil, he saw earth being flung up towards the sky in wild arcs. There were two of these arcs, three or four feet between them. Soil and pebbles and mud thick as clay were being shot up into the air twenty feet or so as though by a rapid, earth-moving machine of some kind. But he could hear the deep clicking and echoing exhales that he knew must be the creature's breathing. It was a few hundred feet away, further into this massive wound in the forest floor, and because of a pile of earth between them, he could only see the heaving, quick ink black of some of its skin from where he stood now. He stepped back two paces, hoping beyond all hope that he could do so silently, and wondering if there were any chance that the thing truly did not know he were there. He had found that once he was in its presence, again, once the lively, strong, wicked color of its form was real and breathing the same air he was, he had no power to make the trade of life for answers. He closed his eyes for a moment, hoping that somehow that act would make it vanish, would make the moment be merely a nightmare or a vision, but when he opened them again, he saw an arc of thick, wet dirt shed clumps of itself within ten feet of him. *That dirt was just touching it,* he thought. He took another step backwards with his left foot, and on that step, he slipped, and fell down into the new dirt floor of the place on his left side, making the sound a flapjack would on a wet skillet. He

Chapter 25

whimpered something that was not English, and he closed his eyes instinctively and felt all of his courage of curiosity fail him when he heard no more clawing and falling dirt. The thing had stopped digging, and the breathing sound had a rougher note to it, now.

His left shoulder was in the soft dirt, and his head had enough of the stinging pain that even in his panic he registered it. But quickly he made the decision that the only thing he could do was to run and hide somewhere. Within a second, he was up and racing along the ground, and then he heard a sound like a stiff breeze running through close, thick trees, and he was tasting and smelling the earth pressed into his nose and between his lips. He was down on the ground, with what felt like the weight of a horse pressing in on his back, and he opened his mouth instinctively to cry out from the pain to his injured head and his back, but his tongue was pushed down into the dark brown topsoil scattered all over the ravine floor. Before he could figure any piece of what was happening to him, he felt a swiftly moving hand against his left side. He could tell, from the pressure and strength against his left set of ribs as the fingers jostled against shirt, that the hand was as large as his chest. He prayed something silently, though in his life he couldn't ever remember believing God would hear his prayers, and then he waited for the blow that would kill him.

Nephilim

At first, Theodore thought the hand was ripping him apart, and that he wasn't feeling it as some sort of protection the flesh can give the mind in moments of agony. But then he realized it was reaching into the pocket of the ripped and dirty suitcoat he was still wearing. The heat of curiosity swept through him again. It was reaching for his knife. This was no thoughtless, mindless beast.

The hand was gone, and he felt the puffy flesh of his belly press into the dirt again. He began to raise his head, believing again that death would be worth seeing the creature, but his head was pushed down into the dirt with such force that he couldn't help screaming. It echoed through the dirt walls of the mud canyon and up over its sides and into the shaded forest, and he had the dim picture in his mind of a man seeing it and coming to his aid. But then he realized the image was of the same man he'd already seen killed by the monster, the man whose ribcage was across the ravine from him. He opened his eyes despite the pain, but couldn't see anything with his head where it was, his right ear being pressed into the ground.

He heard what sounded like the snort of a large animal, and then words.

I have something to show you.

He felt himself picked up, and then felt air and speed as he was carried up out of the ravine and off into the woods. He closed his eyes tightly and

Chapter 25

screamed. But then he felt himself getting sick as the speed with which he was being carried through the shadows increased, and everything seemed to blur around the edges as he fainted.

When Theodore awoke, he was in a cave. His skin felt sensitive to every inch of cool air, and his heart was beating much too quickly. He felt as though he were falling from a great height, and that death and whatever judgment awaited him beyond it was only seconds away. He smelled wet soil coming off the creature, or perhaps dead foliage. Its bulk was visible enough by outline in the sparse light of the place to see that it was about the size of a very, very large bear. He seemed to be outside of himself as he waited for the pain and death, but then the creature finally grabbed the back of his head with the dexterity of a man and forced it to the left, further into the shadow.

He thought from the chalky, damp smell that his face was up against limestone. But it still felt as though another body were undergoing the manipulation. Then a flame sparked behind him and he saw a white wax candle come up against his face from the right, and his mind began to settle back into the reality of his situation. The creature's left hand was still holding his head, but he saw the right hand now, gently wrapped around the new candle. Its skin was mostly coal black, but there were scores across it of grey or white, and for a few seconds he considered them as stripes, but as he looked at them more closely, he realized they were marks of age and use, like wrinkles or scars. He could tell from the texture that surrounded them, the dryness and tightness of the flesh. The hand, when stretched out, would be nearly the size of his own upper body. The candle seemed a ridiculous item seen in it. But then the hand brought it to a spot just above and to the right of Theodore's head, a spot on the wall of the cave where a red drawing was etched on the surface of the stone. It was scrawled with little human ability, and yet it still struck Theodore as somehow intentionally deranged. Perhaps the fact that the head on one of two figures was grossly oversized. But after a moment of studying it, he gathered what he was looking at. A drawing in some red ink or chalk of a man stabbing another in his face. His heart seemed to slide down into his belly and he felt the urge to vomit. The hand tightened on his head, and he heard a wet, smacking sound, as though a sheet of paper had just been slowly lifted off the surface of a sticky table. Then he felt his face drawn to the right, and the sound again but louder and in his right ear. And then he felt pressure and blinding, hot pain on the right side of his neck as the creature took a bite of his flesh just behind his right ear.

He tightened his body and lifted up his right arm to thrash or punch in defense, but he was being crushed against the firmness of the thing's flesh, which through his clothing felt nearly as hard as the shell of a turtle.

Chapter 25

And while he kicked his legs as hard as he could, they found only air; he had been pulled back from the wall of the cave now. His thoughts were charged, wild horses let loose in his mind. This couldn't be happening. But it was happening. Why was it happening? He wondered how he could survive pain that sharp, and then once the creature's teeth pulled back, he fought with every stroke of every muscle he had to protect the wound on his neck but found himself still totally immobile. Then he was up in the air again, and moving, though much more slowly, and further into the darkness.

He tried once to punch into the deepening shadows above him at where he thought the creature's head must be, but he was squeezed with an intensity he didn't think was possible without being killed. The pain left him seeing bright spots, pulsing and making small orbits in what was now thick darkness, and he must have sustained some injury because it persisted throughout their movement further into the cave.

Just as he sensed that they were descending, his gut and inner ears being much more capable of discerning direction than he'd previously known, he sensed heat and saw light. For the briefest of moments, he thought it was a delusion from his injuries, but then he saw the familiar rolling and cresting and flickering that he knew as firelight, and he settled in himself that there was indeed a fire somewhere near them and further down. He couldn't move, as the creature was still holding him much too tightly, and his neck felt as if it had tiny embers of charcoal that would never go out scattered across it where the thing had taken a bite out of him, so he doubted he would be able to turn his head much even if he were free to do so.

When the light was all around him it took a moment for his eyes to adjust. He was still having difficulty thinking from the nervous animation of his mind during the pain and from the weariness and darkness of the trip down into this place. But once he was able to gather up what mental faculties he could in proper order, he could tell even from his position that there were dull shadows dancing in the moving glow, and that the place was mostly lit. He was, he presumed, in a cavern of bewildering size, with some form of firelight in its center.

There were drawings on the wall. Despite the hot pain in his neck, and the ache that was beginning to spill out from it down towards his shoulder, and the pains in his midsection and head, the reality of what he could now see was drawing him in with speed and gravity that woke him up fully. What was this place? What were these things? Had this monster made all of these little sketches as he had, presumably, the one he'd seen earlier? And if so, why?

Suddenly he was on the ground, and his hunger to know what he was looking at evaporated as the pain

Chapter 25

of his drop blinded him and he screamed. The ache from the open wound on his neck was body-wide now that he'd hit the ground, and all of his muscles seemed to be shredded as he rolled over onto his side. Then he opened his eyes and he saw the creature standing in front of him, and he gasped.

It was larger than he had thought, just as a grizzly or a lion strikes men as much larger than they'd thought when they are close enough to smell it, or to see a flea scurrying on its wet nose. He had felt the toughness of its flesh, he'd been injured and even chewed by it, but that had all had happened in the dark, and there was a part of his mind that simply didn't have a template for something this hulking that breathed and moved and ate. He had never killed or even seen a large predatory animal. And of course, he knew this was no animal. It simply wasn't a man.

The first things it said to him were guttural sounds, and he knew they were words merely because each successive sound was so different from the prior. Snorting didn't have vowels. His fascination was food for it, it seemed to him. Because it tilted its head to its right and narrowed its eyes slightly. Theodore didn't know he was standing up until the blood finding its level in his body caused his head and neck to feel as though they were being scorched. But he finished standing. It didn't move as he did. It registered him as he would have a stray cat.

The orange light from the fire behind him cast some sense of space in the cavern. Before he had any understanding of why he was moving, he had been thrown up against the wall that had been to his left. It was smoothed, powdery rock, and he hadn't been thrown hard by the creature, but everything hurt, and he'd cried out much louder than might be expected. He opened his eyes once the sharp pain in all the muscles dissipated, and he saw that it was looking with its oversized black head at one of the etchings in the surface of the wall. Theodore had to know why before he died and had to know what this thing was. It was an affection in his soul that drowned out even his physical pain, which would have surprised him if he had a moment to consider it. He was in agony, and yet this fascination, this curiosity, was a thunderstorm in his heart that fiercely flooded out every other concern. How was it possible that this giant, violent, hard, black, speaking thing that could dig tunnels and hollow out caverns and run faster than Theodore had thought was possible be? How did it exist?

He looked up at the drawing, and as he did, he asked it.

"What are you?"

It looked into him suddenly, and Theodore actually fell to the floor in fear. He could tell it understood him, and he was terrified at the anger its yellowed eyes showed as they squinted in the fire lit

Chapter 25

shadows. It was insane, he decided. He knew it then. And the fear that came with understanding that the thing was irrational was much sharper than when he thought it was a supernatural force personified. A dark angel of some kind might at least be predictable. But a thinking, talking, rabid giant was a much different proposition.

An orphan, it said to him, in a voice that sounded thick and aged. Theodore felt himself wanting to hide under anything he could find, but he couldn't look away from the thing. Its skin seemed jagged and older than rock, and he knew the strength of its hands and limbs, and he knew now it was demented just as it was furious. His face was flush with awe and terror and curiosity that stretched the span of his soul. When he was a boy he had once almost stepped on a copperhead snake in the short grass near his father's back porch, and the feeling he'd had in his chest and arteries and right behind his eyes felt very much like how he felt now. He wanted to run, but he couldn't take his eyes off of it. He felt himself tensing to back up, slowly, but he couldn't do that, either. He was afraid of more pain and of a death that involved his being torn or chewed or crushed, and yet this was the most strangely beautiful thing he had ever seen, and he had to see it for as long as he could.

It breathed out in one of the snorts he had heard several times, now, and then it showed him the images on the walls. Most were deep red and were impossible to make out between the degradation of whatever the substance used to make them had been and the dim light of the fire burning in the middle of the cavern, but several were green, and two were azure. It spoke to him in English that seemed uncomfortable, like a man wearing someone else's clothes, and at the beginning Theodore's heart beat faster and faster and his hands sweat profusely at the unmistakable sound of words coming out of its mouth, this dark, walking thing of muscle and violence that evoked in his nerves all the same effects a beast would have and yet had a mind much like a man's. And as the pain grew hotter and worked its way through all of his muscles, he had trouble standing. As he was looking at the fourth image and hearing it tell him of the young man it showed, Theodore put his hand out to lean on the wall, and was sure he would retch from the pain, but when his hand touched the soft brown rock, he heard the whir of its fastest movements and felt heaved up into the air. He was able to open his eyes and look down at its rage for a moment. Then he was dreaming.

* * *

The first dream was a nightmare. It was unspeakably cold. He felt chill down in his belly, invading his mouth and nose and eyes, making his ears feel as though they

Chapter 25

were being tugged off his head. But it was a living cold, not merely the absence of heat. And the light was even more offensive. It was white and blinding and seemed to gleam, and the fear as he realized how much that light showed about him was almost as painful as his skin and bones against the cold. More painful, actually, as the nightmare drew on and on for what felt like years. He was being examined. Every cowardly, sniveling misdeed he'd ever committed, since the time when he was four-years-old when he slapped the back of his older sister's leg so hard she cried and had loved every minute of her pain, all of it was bare now, and out here in the light of this star and exposed to this chill that was raging through every atom of his nerves.

The second dream was about his father.

* * *

Theodore knew from what it had told him that the world had been a lonelier place when it had been born. He knew now what kinds of things it wanted. But he was a different man an hour after waking up, alone in the shifting orange light of the wood fire the monster had kept burning for what must have been ages. Different and altogether new. The truest thing about God's world is that He made it, and the truest thing about redeemed men is that God has redeemed them. A trust was kindled in Theodore McCabe that night, and all the fuel and the fire and the spark had come from the grace of a Jesus Christ he'd known of quite well as a boy.

* * *

I never knew who Marvin Branson was until the day after I murdered him. Down there in that place that smelled like wet rock and had the monster's awful pictures of what it wanted to do to the world all scratched into its brown limestone. Limestone is water rock. God shed water all over this globe He crafted and spins for us to be on, and He did it because of evil as violent as this monster's, evil as violent as mine against Marvin. The water was life when it was river and rain, but when our folk and the rebel angels had ripped at His world too deeply, He made it judgment, and it washed all the monsters away. Most were men, but some were something different, something larger and stronger and wickeder, and they were mighty in their evil. But the wicked things always end up drowning, because this is His world. Somehow, though, this one breathed on, it dug through the mud and the coral, and its craze is always thirstier, year after year. It hates God now more than it did when men lived lives of centuries, more than back when a man built what would save him because God wanted him safe. The monster may have been jealous then, back when Noah's hands were

Chapter 25

gnarled and sweaty because hammering wooden nails in a craft wider and taller than anything your brothers have built is difficult work. That sort of building takes time and sweat and life and faith. The shallow hate this creature had brought up from its old drowned days takes only time and sweat. This monster was bred from rebel angels and wicked women, and while it would live long, it would always struggle under Someone Else's water and eat from His soil.

It lived. All others of its kind died. And its breath and its hatred of all men and women and children were not from God's pleasure as Adam and Eve were. I'd give everything I have to see Adam, now, and his God walking with him in gardens green in a way nothing is green anymore, green with only life and no death. The gardens in our chests die now, and our children and our hopes die, and everything good dies, and the ugliest parts of it are real, though they are false. I never knew until this night that real things could be lies, but I have seen this Nephilim's drawings. It called itself that, just once, and the word seems familiar to me somehow. I have seen its drawings, and I know that it loves to tell lies with real things, and I know that someday it will be drowned by someone better than me. I am going to die tonight. God has shown me that, and He tells no lies. This Nephilim wants to burn Sunbury. But Sunbury is in God's heart and in His story the same way that boatcrafting old man was once, an old man with three

Nephilim

boys. I have seen the sketch in the northwest corner of this cavern, the only one that isn't aged. I know that it wants to set fire to Sunbury and all her sons and daughters tonight. But it only took my new knife. It did not take my only weapon.

My father was a better man than I have yet been. He was a farmer, but that was not all he was. He had three sons, and like Noah he had one who brought a curse on himself. But in this story of Jehovah's I now know that the prayers of a father can have a greater weight than the troubles of his son. I am Christopher McCabe's boy, and I am a murderer, but I have not been left to what I am by rights. Tonight, all my debts have been paid, drowned by the blood of the Christ my father had always hoped I'd one day know. I knew nothing of worth until tonight, when the Maker of everything good and green and alive, the One who drowns monsters and the deadliest of things, showed me who He was, who I am, and who my father was. Christopher McCabe had veins that showed in his hands, hands that were like tree bark, hard and lined with years that lived in one place, and his roots were the prayers and the faith he held for his three boys. Christopher McCabe was a worker of the soil, but I am also his soil, and his work has lasted this long. I am the last of those three boys to come home, and I will never come home to him here, because he is dead from Adam's doubts, dead like all men die, even Noah, who

Chapter 25

survived the flood. And though this monster has outlived Noah, he will not outlive Noah, because life has two shapes, and this monster's flesh has only taken one.

It must have clung to the walls of a sealed cavern in a mountain, or it drifted on the surface of waters miles deep, but it breathed God's air longer than its mother, and it hated everything that was good and innocent and worthwhile. It hates children. It hates prayers. It hates fathers who love their daughters. And it knows, feels in its crafty bones and its fractured head that each month, each full moon and each summer's full heat, brings it closer to the end it would rather die than witness. It would rather eat itself than see us be happy, and I see now from my father's answered prayers that happiness is the end of this long world that was only once drowned.

So I've written what I can on the page that I ripped out of Marvin Branson's book of heretical prayers. There's no talking to the dead. I have been a hand in a game that sucked souls from what might have been hope, and I murdered a man who might have been my brother, and I am writing on a page from a book that he hoped would make him rich. It's a strange world we're on, one where bad men might be rescued from the traps they set, where Ham might be brought onto the ship, where cowards and mockers can be saved. It is a world much wider and deeper and better than this Nephilim wants it to be. This thing wants the world to be dead and void of men and women and their children. It would have loved the flood if it hadn't been for the ark and the rainbow. It hates children. I know how it hates children from the green sketches on the walls. It would have this place be wiped clean of all trees and all doves and all covenants and all men and their families. Our God used life to drown what was violent, and then He put life in the sky and life in the beak of a bird and life in the loins of His sons to show what His intent was, but this coal monster's heart hates everything that would breathe, everything that would pray, everything that would worship under sunlit sky with clouds spreading thin and color being turned into bow so that we would know promises are at the heart of the story we are in.

I am my father's son. He gave me this knife when we walked out by the pond on our neighbor's property in a July night of black velvet sky, a night when I was thirteen and hoped the world would be better than I thought it was, a night when I wondered whether there were mysteries in girls or in song or in wider spaces in the west that would tell me what this place was and where I should be in it. I had no idea that the ground I was on was once two miles under thick water meant to undo the hatred of liars like this last one out in these woods, but my father gave me this ivory-handled knife, and he told me what to do with it if I ever came across

Chapter 25

a coyote or a bear that did attack. He showed me with his wrists, and his black hair matted to his forehead was wisdom and love and everything I hated and wanted. But in this awful place, the God I now know, the God of my father, the God who has pardoned every wicked thing my violent heart has wanted and has chosen, He has shown me what I might hold that knife for.

That monster has the one I murdered Marvin with. It doesn't have my father's.

* * *

Theodore took the ivory knife back up out of the cave, and despite the fire in every inch of his body, he made his stumbling way to town. It had set a single blaze in the new night, and he saw it huddling underneath the flames licking the frame of a low window. He had forgotten how big it was again, and he wondered if that's how it always worked.

His head and neck had the sharp, hot pain of an infection that is a few hours away from killing a man, but he willed himself to run, and when it turned its ugly face to him, he plunged the blade into its neck as hard as if he were trying to stab a mountainside, and it tried to howl but could only whisper and sputter in pain. Theodore felt himself trying to choke it, and he had a moment to pray before it put its strength and its anger

Nephilim

on him, and Theodore McCabe saw darkness before he saw light.

It stumbled into the woods before falling asleep, doing what healing it could in darkness and in ages.

26
1892

Rachel opened her eyes, and there in the scattered sheets of lantern light was her father. He was holding a white knife, one she had never seen before. Hannibal wasn't moving, and the rifle he'd have used to kill her was laying across his dead right forearm. She felt Mrs. Tufts' hand on her left shoulder, and then looked up again at her father. She had never known how much a father weighed until then. She looked into his dark eyes and wondered whether he were something different than she had feared, something harder and safer than she had conceived the world could hold, and she crashed her hull against the hardness of his rocks, and her tears made the collars of his white shirt dark gray, and she hoped this was what the world was. Raymond, her father, his collarbone on her forehead, his strength on her faith, his depth on her hopes.

* * *

After Raymond had cut its throat, it threw him through the air and then tumbled down a slope just to their right. By the time he'd stood up, he heard one more howl far away in the west. He'd tried to follow, but even dying it was much too fast for him. And then he'd heard, back in the direction of town, what sounded like a rifle shot and a woman's scream, and he'd run back, afraid of what he'd find. He never discovered the spot where it finally fell. But he did find Josiah. He was able to lay him to rest in Sunbury soil.

Rachel Stanton was a special woman. Her heart was wide and thick. She adopted Noel Flagler's boys when his wife died of the same fever that took Mrs. Atwood, that took Rachel's own mother, and she raised them up as men of faith as heavy and brave as that of her father's. Those two boys became Reverend Lowells in their own right, men who took the world to be a special place filled with what might be saved from its potential. Noel Flagler's boys became Rachel Stanton's sons, and Rachel Stanton's sons became the crossbourne missionaries of a world to come. The older of the two died of malaria at the Yangtze River's southeastern most bend. He was under a willow tree where Hudson Taylor had once prayed a prayer as old and wide as a Redwood. "Send someone, God. Send someone." God did, because He is a wise and good God, and this is His world, and no army of devil-bred monsters will breathe one foul whisper against the story He intends to tell with it. The other son died in Sunbury. He took over Reverend Lowell's church, thirteen years after the old man had died on the night the night the monster did. The night when Raymond Stanton found what he'd hoped could still be around in a world without his wife.

Chapter 26

Most of Sunbury remained convinced through the years that something from the woods had shed blood those few nights in their town, though as time wore on with no more disturbances some contended Hannibal Guthridge had somehow been the chief culprit. Only Rachel Stanton, Raymond Stanton, and Abigail Tufts were ever sure that some sort of hateful thing had long stalked Sunbury's woods in hopes to drown something good it sensed would come. They knew it meant something, and so Abigail Tufts would sometimes look at Rachel Stanton and her two adopted sons and smile, and remember how deep this world could get.

Rachel Stanton prayed every Psalm over the older of her two boys, at least one every day until he found himself on that ship to the other part of her globe, and she sang the same hymn almost every night to both of them. She spilled a love and faith over boys born to Noel Flagler that would certainly have made him wonder whether the world was a place of more promise than he'd once thought.

Rachel was a woman of deeper and better things than the monster who sought her blood. I know it, though both of them are buried now. I know it when things seem darker than they should be.

Nephilim